MOST DEFINITELY MURDER

Mrs. Lillywhite Investigates
BOOK SIX

EMILY QUEEN

Most Definitely Murder

First Edition

Printed in the U.S.A.

Table of Contents

CHAPTER ONE

Rosemary Lillywhite searched the roadway for a black auto, or more specifically, a black auto manned by a rugged, six-foot-tall, sandy-haired man. Several of the ones parked along the side of the high street matched the description, but she couldn't find her butler, Wadsworth, among them.

"Well, he must have got caught up circling the block," she said with defeat to her dearest friend, Vera Blackburn. "Why don't we just walk and see if we come across him."

"It isn't as if we're laden with shopping bags," Vera grudgingly agreed. "The shops don't seem to have much in the way of tempting wares today." It was unlike Vera not to find at least one item to strike her fancy, and Rosemary sighed as the cloud that had been circling her friend's head all day grew darker still.

"Out with it," Rose demanded, beginning to stroll and pulling Vera along with her. "What on earth is bothering you?"

Vera hemmed and hawed for a few moments, her stride quickening, and finally threw her hands in the air. "My wedding is turning into a disaster! Our mothers have gone entirely insane. I fear by the time they're done, it will be the most ostentatious event of the century!"

"You must have known that when you decided to marry my brother, Mother was included in the deal," Rosemary reminded her. Evelyn Woolridge was a force of nature, certainly, and she'd become even more tightly wound in recent months. After a murder had taken place at Woolridge House—a murder Rosemary and Vera had helped solve—it seemed a fire had been lit under Evelyn. With her efforts focused solely on the impending nuptials, she was driving Vera mad.

"Now," Rosemary mused, "she's going toe-to-toe with your mother, and everyone knows Lorraine Blackburn throws the best parties. I'll bet Mother simply doesn't want to be outdone."

Uncharacteristically, Vera snapped at Rosemary. "Yes, that much has become abundantly clear. Mother's guest list has exceeded a hundred and fifty names, and she refuses to cut it to a more reasonable number. Evelyn, concerned the aisles will be lopsided, has expanded her list, and now you and Frederick have long lost cousins coming out of the woodwork."

Vera threw her hands in the air in frustration. "The last time my mother called, she couldn't decide whether we ought to choose a six-piece band or a string quartet, and I left her musing over hiring both and a great harpist besides."

Rosemary nearly chuckled, but Vera's expression of despair cured her of the inclination. "It sounds like a perfectly lovely party, aside the pop-up cousins, of course."

"You're not nearly as funny as you think you are, Rosie. The worst part is that my mother wants me to wear her dress." Vera's tone now verged on hysterical. "It's positively hideous, and she didn't even ask if I wanted it. She just assumed I'd be thrilled, and if I tell her the truth, she'll be crushed."

Vera's statement, combined with something Rosemary spotted further down the street, caused her to yank hard on Vera's arm.

"Ouch! Honestly, Rose, I don't know what's got into you, but you're hurting me!"

"Pish posh!" Rosemary retorted in a fair imitation of Evelyn. "I've just figured out our first plan of attack. Now, come on," she said, pointing to the window of a dress shop where several fancy frocks hung on display. "We're going to find you the perfect, understated dress, and we'll force both our mothers to design the rest of the wedding fete around it!"

Stopping dead in her tracks, Vera viewed the offerings and raised one eyebrow. "None of those are really my style, Rosie," she said, backing away from the door. "They look suspiciously similar to the dress I already have no interest in wearing."

"You look as though I've just asked you to dive into a vat of boiling acid," Rosemary laughed, "rather than to participate in your favorite pastime of spending money on new clothes. Besides, I'm sure they have more styles hidden away, and if you don't find anything you like, then we'll visit every shop in London until you do. The dress always determines the type of wedding you're going to have. We can head our mothers off right here and avoid much of the fuss."

Rose only half-believed the assurances with which she showered her friend, knowing full well it would take nothing less than a miracle to convince either Evelyn Woolridge or Lorraine Blackburn to tone down their plans. It was worth a shot even if she succeeded only in raising Vera's spirits.

Vera glared at Rosemary and crossed her arms resolutely. Undeterred, Rose hauled her inside, forcefully, where the slightly musty scent of linens not entirely covered by that of rose potpourri caused Vera's nose to wrinkle. Perhaps, Rose thought, she'd been wrong about this endeavor after all, but she made a conscious effort to breathe through her mouth and carried on as though the notion hadn't crossed her mind.

Almost immediately, a lively shopgirl descended upon the pair. "Hello, ladies. Which of you is the bride-to-be?" she asked, smiling. Her buoyant mood deflated somewhat at the sight of Vera's thinly pressed lips, and she shifted her gaze to Rosemary.

"My name is Rosemary, and this is my friend Vera," Rose explained, digging her elbow into Vera's ribs as a reminder to mind her manners. "Who is to be wed."

With an eye roll, Vera pasted a smile on her face. "Yes, I'm in need of a dress, but I don't as yet know precisely what style I want."

"Well, that's no trouble," the girl trilled, her sunny smile having returned. "We have a number of options, and of course, we can make alterations if you find a silhouette that appeals to you. I'll be back with some selections, and we can go from there," she said, eying Vera's slim figure with just a touch of envy.

Vera mumbled a thank you, then avoided Rosemary's gaze and wandered around the shop. She turned up her nose at a selection of Juliet Cap veils in one corner, her attention taken by a display of diamanté headpieces. "That one would look lovely on you," Rose said softly, pointing at a particularly lovely example, knowing her friend wouldn't be able to commit to a melancholy mood in the presence of so many sparkling baubles.

"Of course it would," Vera retorted, sticking her nose in the air for a fraction of a second before she caved, and her lips cracked into a smile.

Leaving Vera to browse, Rosemary loitered near an abandoned rack and fingered the lace of a dress bodice that reminded her of her own wedding. Thinking about that day should have been a reason to smile, but drew a frown from her instead. It had been just over a year since she'd lost her husband Andrew, suddenly, due to an undetected heart problem. Even though she'd begun to pick up the pieces of her decimated life and move on, the pain still had a way of coming back with such vengeance it sometimes caught her off guard. Tears welled in her eyes, and she brushed them away impatiently. Ruining Vera's first foray into wedding planning would not resolve the situation, and she had no intention of taking away even a piece of her dearest friend's happiness.

"All right then," the shopgirl called out, interrupting Rosemary's reverie. "I've pulled several dresses I think might suit your fancy." She appeared well relieved when she noticed Vera's demeanor had changed from irritation to moderate interest. "Why don't you try this one first?" she asked, holding out a voluminous tuft of satin and tulle with what appeared to be a nearly ten-foot-long train.

The reprieve didn't last because Vera took one look at it and her expression reverted back to a scowl. "Absolutely not," she crossed her arms resolutely and refused to budge.

When the poor girl had once again retreated into the back following Vera's veto of the rest of the selections, Rose—her sadness having dissolved—whirled on her friend and dished out a rare tongue lashing.

"I don't know who you are, but you need to bring back my friend. My friend who would never speak to a shopgirl the way you just did. Really, Vera, you're acting positively horrendously!"

There wasn't time for Vera to retort because something across the room had caught her eye. She marched up to the till counter and picked up a framed photograph that had been resting on top. "This is it. This is the dress I want," she said, turning the picture around so Rosemary could appraise it.

"It's beautiful," Rosemary breathed after a few quiet moments. Beautiful, it was; a simple sheaf of snowy white satin covered in hand-beaded embroidered lace, with a cinched waist and a short, ruffled train. "Not exactly of the current style, but still modern and at the same time rather classic somehow. Yet, I wouldn't call it understated. This dress is a showpiece, and choosing it would give our mothers even more ammunition for throwing the ball of the century. Nevertheless, it's absolutely perfect for you!"

A genuine smile broke out across Vera's face then. "Even Mother would have to agree this gown is more appropriate than her old frock. Perhaps all hasn't been lost."

When the shopgirl reappeared, a few strands of hair stuck up on end, and her cheeks were flushed, but she'd gathered several more frocks for Vera's inspection.

"Oh, we don't need to look at any more. I've found the one I want," Vera explained, prompting the poor girl's face to twitch with the effort of holding back an irritated scowl. She held up the photograph and was met with a furrowed brow.

"I'm terribly sorry, but that's simply not possible," the girl replied.

9

Vera smiled. "Money is no object in this case. I'll pay handsomely, you can rest assured."

"Oh no, you misunderstand. It isn't a matter of cost," the girl replied. "You see, the dressmaker who made it has, unfortunately, passed away. That was the last dress he made, and it was for his daughter. I'm sure our new seamstress can craft something comparable. She'll be in this afternoon if you'd like to schedule a consultation."

"Hmm," Vera murmured under her breath, her eyes still trained on the picture of the dress. "I'll let you know, shall I?" Her shoulders slumped, and she left the shop looking very much like a forlorn child.

Rose elbowed Vera gently in the ribs. "Why not speak to the seamstress? What can it hurt?" she wanted to know.

"There's no use, Rosie. Whoever made those atrocious dresses—an insult to fashion, I tell you— isn't capable of the kind of work I'm looking for. That photograph has ruined everything." It wasn't unlike Vera to resort to dramatics. She was, after all, an actress, as Rose was forced to remind herself while she sighed and rolled her neck to relieve some of the tension that had settled there.

When they exited to the street to find Wadsworth standing by the car, Rosemary let out a sigh of relief. "How did you know where to find us?" she asked.

"Lucky guess, Miss," Wadsworth replied, though his usual cheerful demeanor seemed to have vanished. "Though I would have preferred not to have been forced to hunt you two ladies down. These are dangerous times we're living in, and the streets aren't safe," he pointed out, his voice full of overprotective concern.

The point well taken, Rosemary apologized. "We didn't mean to alarm you, but surely we're safe here on the high street, surrounded by throngs of other shoppers."

"That's not a risk I'm willing to take," Wadsworth replied, proving that Andrew's confidence in his abilities had been well-earned. It was he who had hired Wadsworth, accepting no other applications for the job. Rose found that since Andrew's passing, she'd come to appreciate his selection of butler more than she'd ever thought possible.

"Where is your haul?" Wadsworth indicated the open boot and looked around with a bewildered expression on his face.

"No bags today, Wadsworth," Vera said sullenly. "We didn't find what we were looking for."

Wadsworth's lip quirked—he'd always had a soft spot for Vera, and vice versa—but he merely closed the boot and winked at her, his irritation having ebbed. "Don't blame the shops for not being able to offer up anything comparable to your exquisiteness."

Try as she might, there wasn't a thing Vera could do to suppress the smile that spread across her face. She patted Wadsworth on the back as he held open the car door and planted a kiss on his cheek. "You're one in a million, Wads. Don't ever change."

"I don't plan on it, Miss Blackburn."

Chapter Two

"Here's one, my love," Frederick said through a bite of muffin. "Four bedrooms, servant's quarters, and a terrace overlooking the river." He laid the morning paper back down on the table to take a sip of steaming tea and gazed at Vera indulgently. "It's quite pricey, of course," he added cheerfully.

At that, Rosemary stifled a snort. She would never understand how her brother and Vera, who had known each other since birth, had only recently realized they belonged together. Two peas in a pod, they were, and it had taken twenty-some-odd years for either of them to notice.

Vera shrugged off the financial concern with a roll of her eyes, just as Rose had expected she might. She picked up the paper, her fingers brushing Fred's lovingly as she did so, and tossed a dazzling smile in his direction. "It's right around the corner! Rosie, we'd be neighbors!"

Frederick smiled again and wiggled his eyebrows at his sister. "She'll be sick of us by Boxing Day, I'm quite certain."

Standing near the door, Wadsworth suppressed a grin while Rosemary's brow furrowed. She wondered if she ought to remind Frederick that she'd recently begun to consider moving out of the townhouse. Lately, the home she'd shared with Andrew felt much too spacious for one person to rattle about in it alone. "Wait just a moment," she said, having finally processed the meaning behind her brother's statement. "The wedding isn't until February, long after Boxing Day."

Fred and Vera exchanged a meaningful glance, and then he turned back to Rose with his eyes sparkling mischievously. "We're bunking tradition and moving in together as soon as we find a suitable house. Vera's already given up her flat, effective at the end of the month, and I'll be stationed at the London offices full-time from here on out. So you see, we're on a time crunch, although I'm sure if we can't find what we're looking for, you'll kindly allow Vera to stay on here."

A firm supporter of the changing times, she wasn't in the least scandalized by Frederick's statement, but Rosemary raised an eyebrow anyway. "Of course. You two have practically been living here anyway, and I adore having you around. My bigger concern is whether Mother and Father know about your plans to live together in sin," she smirked. "Presumably, they do not, since I haven't received word from the morgue that Mother's head has exploded."

Vera shrugged off the comment, though her eyes turned cloudy at the thought of her future mother-in-law's reaction to the news. Frederick merely shook his head wryly, a small smile indicating his low level of concern, and went back to perusing the advertisements. Rosemary decided the pair of them could deal with Evelyn's wrath on their own and dispensed with the discussion altogether. Instead, she picked up the sheets he'd discarded and sighed as she read through the headlines.

As it had been for the last two weeks, news of an escaped murderer dominated the front page. Rosemary shivered and read aloud, *"Garrison Black, convicted mass murderer, continues to evade capture. According to Commissioner Gibson of the London constabulary, Black escaped while awaiting imminent execution."*

Rosemary studied the dark-eyed, bearded man pictured below the headline, a shiver chasing across her skin.

"To date, Black has brutally slain at least six unmarried, flaxen-haired, females between the ages of seventeen and twenty. Black's arrest followed an investigation which turned up the following facts: Black chose his victims carefully, watching each one for weeks and lying in wait until such time as he could enter their homes unseen. He concealed himself inside and waited for his victims to return, whereupon he beat the women brutally before shooting them in the heart and leaving them for dead.

"The search for Black began during his first spate of murders ten years ago, which was followed by a period of latent years. Black's return six years ago resulted in several more deaths, including that

of one London policeman. Again, Black eluded arrest until two months ago when officers were finally able to track and apprehend the fugitive. Unfortunately, Black escaped a London jailhouse two weeks ago and is still in the wind."

"It goes on to say that Black leaves a calling card. An actual card with some sort of symbol on it—there's no photograph—and that *Commissioner Gibson advises extreme caution, as Black is believed to have gone to ground somewhere in or around London, where all of his previously known murders were committed."*

Wadsworth interrupted Rosemary's oration with a snort. "If he were as smart as he thinks he is, he'd get out of London as fast as he can. Until he does, I must insist that you ladies do not leave this house without an escort."

"I second that recommendation," Frederick said with a pointed look at Vera, who pressed her lips together, and for once remained silent.

Having no intention of disobeying Wadsworth's request, Rosemary continued reading. "'The officer who apprehended Black will be honored for his service at the annual Fallen Heroes

Banquet tomorrow night.' Drat," Rosemary stopped reading and looked up from the paper.

"I'd nearly forgotten about the banquet. I suppose there's no getting out of it, as I've already told Max I'd attend as his guest. Though come to think of it, I've not heard him mention it again since he asked."

Furthermore, she'd seen neither hide nor hair of Maximilian Whittington for near on a week, and the admission wasn't one she cared to make aloud. Most likely, he had probably become embroiled in the search for Garrison Black, or at least that's what Rosemary told herself.

In truth, she'd felt tension between them ever since the pair had reluctantly admitted to having romantic feelings for one another. Reluctantly was the operative word, and it kept flitting through Rosemary's thoughts like a gnat. She wouldn't have been the first widow to fall in love with her dead husband's best mate, but that didn't make the situation any more socially acceptable. Andrew and Max had started out as constables together, and though Andrew's enthusiasm for the work had eventually waned, Max hung in and moved quickly up the ranks.

Rosemary had been confident his professed feelings were genuine, and whether complicated or not, she hadn't regretted her own admission. Perhaps Max hadn't felt the same; it was possible he'd had second thoughts and didn't know how to let her down easy.

"Didn't they already honor Andrew?" Frederick asked sharply.

He'd been the one to escort his sister to the banquet the previous year. It had been mere weeks after Andrew's unexpected death, and Frederick could still recall the haunted expression that had paled Rosemary's face throughout the entire evening. "Sounds to me as though you've suffered enough."

The subject of Black's escape had been all anyone could talk about lately and had dominated the breakfast conversation each morning since the first news hit the headlines. That on this day, the topic had shifted to Rosemary's personal life spoke volumes regarding Frederick's concern for her well-being.

Rose shot her brother a quelling look. "Yes, he was mentioned last year, even though his tenure as an officer ended nearly two years before. I thought it quite lovely for him to still be remembered fondly." At this, Wadsworth loosed a muffled grunt that caused Rosemary to gaze at him with a question in her eyes. He duly ignored her unvoiced inquiry, and it occurred to Rosemary that perhaps it was the mention of Andrew that had caused her butler to wince.

"This has been the first year to pass unmarked by a single death—quite unprecedented, I'm assured," she continued. "The focus will shift towards those officers who have provided exemplary service."

"Yes, Rosie, I read the article," Frederick began. "Nathaniel Prescott will be honored for his service, including the apprehension of Garrison Black, which is, evidently, what won him the boost from constable to sergeant. If you want my opinion, with Black on the loose, a celebration hardly seems appropriate. There's a whole section that describes Prescott's virtues at great length and with boundless enthusiasm. My recommendation is that you read it, skip the event altogether, and move on with your life."

Of course, that would be Frederick's advice. The Woolridge family motto might as well have been *take all your feelings and sweep them under the rug*, but Rose had long since realized in that sense at least, she was happy to pave her own path.

"I have to go, Freddie. Max is finally receiving his promotion to chief inspector. It's been months since Inspector Crowley was divested of his title, and Max was promoted. There have been several delays, and he has yet to be officially named as Crowley's successor. It's important to him, and therefore I will go whether I want to or not."

She picked the newspaper back up and looked at the photo of Nathaniel Prescott. A broad forehead sat below a head of thick, dark hair and a pair of perfectly shaped brows. A set of fine lines around his eyes indicated he was a man who smiled widely and often. Rose vividly remembered him from her experience as a fellow cop's wife, though she had to admit he had a face *no* woman was likely to forget.

"I'll be fine, Freddie. I'll be with Max," Rosemary said as if that ended the discussion. Her brother opened his mouth to challenge her, but Vera silenced him with a glare.

"You don't think Evelyn will really be angry about our plans, do you?" Vera asked, returning the subject to her impending nuptials. Rose suspected images of lace and lilies cycled through her best friend's mind on an unending loop these days. "Perhaps we ought to consider moving up the wedding, after all, Freddie."

With a raised eyebrow, Frederick attempted to quell her fears. "Mother will be just fine, and we've Father on our side. He'll handle her. However, if you'd rather skip the pomp and circumstance, we can go down to the registry office and tie the knot anytime you like."

The suggestion seemed to pique Vera's interest. "It wouldn't be the worst thing in the world, and it would end the madness of wedding planning quite neatly. I wouldn't have to set eyes on that atrocious gown of Mother's ever again. In fact, we could take things one step further and simply elope to a tropical island to be wed beneath the palm fronds," she continued to muse, leaving Rosemary no doubt it wasn't the size or ostentatiousness of the event to which her friend objected. No, Vera merely wished to choose her own ensemble and now that she hadn't got her way, decided the best way out was to simply call the whole thing off.

While Frederick's eyes lit up at the prospect, Rosemary's darkened ominously. "If you're trying to stay on Mother's good side, I wouldn't recommend robbing her of the joys of wedding planning altogether. Particularly the wedding of her favorite child."

The statement fell like a stone, as the three of them knew good and well it had been their brother Lionel who'd carried that title. Had he not been killed, tragically, in the war, it would have been his and Vera's wedding in question. Rosemary felt as though she'd put her foot in her mouth, as Vera's attachment to Lionel was the real reason it had taken her several years to warm up to Frederick in the first place.

"Yes, well," Vera said, sidestepping the gaffe even as Rose's face pinked, "our relationship couldn't possibly get any worse."

Rosemary quirked a brow, "You seem to be suffering from selective memory, Vera dear. You and Mother are finally on a firm footing. It simply wouldn't do to pull the rug from beneath her now. Why don't we do a little digging with regards to that perfect dress, and if nothing comes of it, we'll discuss alternative options."

Vera agreed though she appeared skeptical, and Frederick rolled his eyes but didn't argue. It was the best Rosemary could hope for, and so she let the subject return to possible house options and nibbled her scone in silence until the cook exited the kitchen door in a flurry.

She began clearing the dishes, taking Fred's saucer out from under the teacup he had pressed to his lips. He looked up, surprised, and raised an eyebrow in a near mirror image of the expression Rosemary had peered at Vera with only moments before.

"Helen, where is Mrs. Moore?" Rose asked, keeping her voice even. While her mother—the famous Evelyn—might have kicked up a fuss, she had decided long ago she wouldn't stoop to that level with her own staff.

The cook, Helen, snapped, "Had an appointment with the doctor, she did. Left me to do her job as well as my own. And I suppose, since Wadsworth has disappeared, I'll be left in charge of the telephone as well. He's received several messages this week and won't deign to answer even a single one."

Rosemary's head swung to and fro, for she hadn't noticed her butler's departure. "I'm sure he'll be back soon. He's probably tending to something in the garage. You'd do well to remember, Helen, that auto repair isn't part of his job description either, just as kitchen work isn't part of Anna's. You won't hear a word of protest from her, even though technically, as my maid, she's only to take care of my personal needs. We all do what we can, and I pay the lot of you handsomely for your time." Her tone was light, but the meaning behind her words struck home, and Helen retreated back into the kitchen without another word.

Once Frederick had left for work and Vera for a rehearsal of her latest play—a lighthearted romantic comedy, for once—Rosemary wandered the townhouse listlessly, discovering Wadsworth was, in fact, nowhere to be found.

She wished she had somewhere to be or that she had pursued an art career after finishing her time at school. Instead, she'd married Andrew and decided she'd rather raise a passel of children. For the five brief years of their marriage, they had tried to make that dream a reality, but it hadn't been in the stars.

Now that he was gone and she'd finally begun to heal, Rosemary realized how empty her life felt. Even though she was still a young woman, the idea of a family was so far out of reach it made her want to cry.

As she perused the portraits of herself and Andrew—just the two of them—that lined the wall above the stairs to the upper floors, her mind kept returning to the plaque he'd had made for her.

Making up her mind, Rosemary descended to the lowest level of the flat where Andrew had operated Lillywhite Investigations after he'd left the police department for less dangerous pursuits. Had he known how little time he had left, or that death would come in the form of an undiagnosed heart problem rather than at the hands of a murder suspect, perhaps he wouldn't have been so intent on changing career paths.

Or, perhaps he would have anyway, Rose decided. When the man had wanted something, he put all of his energy into obtaining it. His pursuit of her affections was case in point, she vividly recalled. Meanwhile, here she was sulking over a dalliance in art that probably would have soured her on the idea of working for a living in the first place. That she'd stalled in the middle of transforming the space from an office into a studio for herself spoke volumes about just how mercurial her temperament had become lately.

Rosemary ignored the stacks of unfinished canvases piled around the rest of the space to opened the top desk drawer and began sifting through the detritus of her husband's last days: a receipt from a dinner at Kettner's from their anniversary; an old watch that had made him late one too many times before being tossed aside in favor of a modern model; and finally a rectangular box that held a gift he hadn't had the chance to give his wife.

Rosemary Lillywhite, Private Investigator, it read. Andrew's faith in her—faith that many men would have ridiculed—still filled her heart with joy. He'd been one in a million, and Rose held no illusions regarding how lucky she'd been to have him in her life, even if only for a limited time.

She delved into the next drawer down, finding a stack of case files she had laid aside the last time she'd tried to clear out the desk. Rose laid the pile aside and ran her palm over the bottom of the drawer to ensure nothing had gone unnoticed. Coming up empty-handed, she took one last look inside and noticed something odd. Upon further inspection, it seemed as if the drawer wasn't as deep as it ought to have been, and so when Wadsworth entered the room, it was to find Rosemary lying on the floor and examining the underside of the desk.

"Couldn't I be of some assistance?" he asked dryly, causing her to sit up suddenly and whack her head against the bottom of the drawer.

"Ouch," she said, rubbing at the spot where her forehead had connected with solid wood. "No, I was perfectly all right," she went on accusingly.

Wadsworth bit back a grin. "I do apologize, madam. Would you like an aspirin?"

"No, thank you," she replied, raising her chin in the air but allowing him to offer her a hand and pull her back to her feet. "However, I would like to know—what exactly did you do to Helen?" Rosemary asked him. The telephone hadn't rung all afternoon, and she hoped that blessing alone would have a positive effect on Helen's mood.

Wadsworth grimaced and appeared somewhat reluctant to explain but changed his mind when Rosemary's expression brooked no refusal. "I'd say all I've done is possess the audacity to do my job—that, and the fact that I'm a man doesn't help. She thinks we're all swine, didn't you know? It's no skin off my nose, but shortly after Andrew hired me on here, I rearranged the flatware drawer, and she's never forgiven me."

Rosemary wondered if that was all there was to it, given Wadsworth's shifty eye, but let the subject drop.

CHAPTER THREE

Max rang that afternoon to confirm his plans with Rosemary, but it didn't quell her fears the way she had expected it to. Something in his tone made her think perhaps he had hoped she would back out of the banquet. Overnight, the thought spiraled into a deep cavern of fear she hadn't realized was there, and she called upon Vera for some good advice while readying herself for the evening.

"Max is a straight shooter if I ever met one," Vera stated with assurance. "If he didn't want to go, he would have said so."

"Perhaps he's lost interest. You know how men are," Rose replied, giving voice to her worries for the first time. "They enjoy the hunt, but then when they actually catch something dither about deciding how to skin the meat."

"That's a cheery comparison," Vera said with a raised eyebrow. "You're not a caught hare, Rosie, and Max is simply besotted with you."

Rose chewed her lip doubtfully. "He seemed to be, certainly, but I've been on the fence. It still feels like it's too soon for me to really fall in love with someone else, and I wouldn't be surprised if Max has picked up on that and decided to maintain a safe distance."

"You know what they say, the best way to get over one man..." Vera wiggled her eyebrows this time and elicited a snarl from her friend that she duly ignored, instead burying her head in Rosemary's wardrobe.

"I think that's only valid when one has been dumped," Rose replied wryly. "I don't believe the adage applies to widows."

Vera sighed. "Yes, well, you may be right there, Rose, but the fact you've managed to develop feelings for him means you're closer to healed than you think you are. Here, wear this." She pulled out a dress in a deep shade of purple and tossed it on the bed. "It's near enough to black to be considered somber, but with a low enough neckline to get Max's heart racing."

Except, when Max arrived, his heart was already racing. A sheen of sweat coated his forehead, and his breath came in gasps. "I suppose...I ought to resume my daily calisthenics...if running five blocks has me winded," he huffed after a cursory hello.

"Why on earth were you running?" Rosemary asked, taking in his now-wrinkled suit and ruddy complexion.

"Damn car...broke down," he explained. "Couldn't get a cab. Trouble you for a drink of water?"

Rosemary withheld a giggle but fetched him what he asked for. He'd removed his jacket and was fanning himself with a discarded evening paper when she found him again in the parlor.

"I'm afraid I'm going to have to keep my coat on all evening," Max said irritably, indicating the underarms of his shirt, which were drenched in sweat.

Without thinking about it, she offered, "You can wear one of Andrew's shirts if you like."

The suggestion hung in the air for a half-second too long before Rose added, "Unless that would be awkward. I'm sorry, perhaps I shouldn't have—"

"No," Max said quickly. "I mean, yes." He sighed. "It's all right, and you shouldn't have not said it. That didn't come out right, either, did it?" Max sighed once more and started over again. "I'd be honored to wear one of Andy's shirts."

"I'll go fetch one then."

The nickname that had tripped off Max's tongue caused a memory Rose had suppressed to resurface. As she climbed the stairs, she allowed it to play through her mind, discovering that the remembrance didn't elicit the sharp pang of pain it once would have. Now, it brought only comfort.

"Andy! For goodness sake, stop trying to pawn me off on all your friends!" Max had admonished after a particularly loathsome evening when Andrew had thought it a good idea to try to pair him up with Vera.

"I want you to be as happy as I am, old chap," Andrew had replied, lavishing a loving gaze on his wife. With a friendly wink in Rosemary's direction, Max had fired back, *"I highly doubt that will ever happen. You got the last good one in all of England."* She'd never dreamed he meant a word

of it, but knowing he'd always thought highly of her buoyed her spirits.

She returned to Max, feeling somewhat more confident in their burgeoning romance than she had before, and handed him the shirt. "I've packed away most of his things, but I thought perhaps I ought to keep back a couple of shirts. Sentimentality, you know," she explained.

"Well, I'm right lucky you did," Max replied with a gentle smile. "Now, do you think Wadsworth would mind driving us tonight? I don't fancy another jog across town, particularly with you in those shoes."

It took a little longer than usual for Wadsworth to arrive in answer to Rosemary's call. When he finally did, his gaze didn't quite meet hers, causing her to wonder if he'd dallied on purpose.

"I know it's your evening off, but would you mind terribly bringing us to the fallen heroes banquet?"

Wadsworth appeared to silently debate his answer but mistakingly made eye contact with his mistress. His expression immediately softened, and he said, "Of course, let me bring the car around."

Spinning on his heel, he made a hasty exit, and a few moments later, Rosemary heard the sounds of an engine roaring to life.

Max stayed quiet during the ride, though he kept Rosemary's hand between his, absentmindedly stroking her fingers every so often. She decided to let him stew over whatever it was that had been holding his attention and instead focused on watching the city lights flash by in a comfortable blur.

"Here we are," Wadsworth said, coming to a stop in the middle of the street. Cars lined the edge of the footway, obscuring any view of the base of the steep steps leading to the reception hall entrance. Another car pulled up next to them, and the driver turned his head in their direction. He did a quick double-take, his eyes darting from Max and Rosemary to Wadsworth, and then smirked as he casually turned his head back the other way. Still, the expression on his face wasn't missed by any of them.

Max made a grunting sound and shook his head in disgust.

"Do you know that man?" Rosemary asked.

"Yes, that was Percy Turner, one of my *colleagues,*" Max explained, his voice colored with disdain. He watched the man exit his vehicle and quickly ascend the stairs, stopping short halfway up. There, a couple stood in front of a set of double doors, conversing with a portly fellow Rosemary recognized as Alfie Gibson, the Commissioner who had been quoted, daily, in all the London papers.

Abruptly, Percy changed his trajectory so that he was as far away from the grouping as he could possibly get by the time he arrived at the top of the stairs.

"What was that about?" Rose asked Max, realizing that half the couple standing with the commissioner consisted of none other than Nathaniel Prescott, the sergeant being honored later in the evening.

"Why don't I just say this: it's a good thing Turner doesn't work in our department anymore. He can't be in the same room with Nate Prescott after a falling out they had a few years ago."

Intrigued, Rose asked, "Over what?"

Max shrugged. "No idea. Neither of them would ever say, so I suspect it had to do with a woman."

Rose's eyes flicked to the one standing next to Mr. Prescott, and her brow furrowed.

"That's Nate's wife, Esme. He married her last year, and she's actually quite a lovely person. At first glance, they make for rather an odd couple, though, don't they?" he said under his breath just before a horn honked behind them. The noise didn't seem to rouse Wadsworth, who was staring at the gathering atop the stairs with an unfathomable expression on his face.

The sound of the horn caught Nathaniel Prescott's attention, and he did a quick scan of the street before his eyes lit upon Rosemary and Max's figures emerging from the car. He nodded in Max's direction, then glanced towards the driver's seat with a raised eyebrow. His hand came up in a half-wave, and he started down the stairs.

Max returned the wave as Wadsworth shooed him and Rosemary away from the car. "I'll return at the end of the evening to collect you," he said.

"No, no, we'll take a cab," Rose assured, to which Wadsworth replied by simply nodding once and pulling quickly away.

Max took her hand and led her up the stairs, giving Rosemary a chance to appraise Mrs.

Prescott. She did appear rather plain—though not unattractive, by any means—standing next to her handsome husband, who in person looked even better than his photo from the paper.

With a glance at Max's profile, Rose idly wondered how this district had come to be filled with the city's best looking officers.

Chapter Four

The hall was sparsely but elegantly dressed in white linens, swags of red and blue lining the stage, with clusters of white roses on every table. Max and Rose were placed next to Alfie and Ivy Gibson, the commissioner and his wife. Rosemary vaguely remembered their kind words from the prior year and recalled that Ivy had been quite friendly towards her on the other few occasions they'd had to meet.

Commissioner Gibson raised an eyebrow as he noted Max's grip on Rose's hand but was gracious enough not to say anything regarding the subject. For such a boisterous man, it must have taken a great deal of self-control. Rosemary reminded herself that restraint was a valuable asset to a cop, and Alfie Gibson hadn't been given the title of Commissioner by default.

"Rosemary, it's so lovely to see you again. You're looking well. I'm glad to see it," Ivy said, standing to deposit a kiss on each of Rose's cheeks. Closing in on her mid-50's, Mrs. Gibson wasn't a beautiful woman by any stretch of the imagination, but there was something commanding about her. Charisma, Rose thought, was something she possessed in spades. She also thought it fortuitous that the commissioner had managed to find a wife who didn't wilt like a wallflower in his overwhelming presence.

"Yes, yes, right so," he said, taking Rose's hand in his two bear-like ones before she'd even had a chance to reply to his wife's greeting. Ivy waved him away and switched chairs so that she could sit closer to Rosemary, and he merely complied without complaining. He did, however, turn to Max and comment that he'd rather be at home, listening to the wireless, than all trussed up in a suit and tie.

"Don't mind him; he's been in a tizzy all day," Ivy winked and whispered to Rose conspiratorially. "I simply can't understand why. Usually, my husband jumps at any chance to show off in front of a crowd." She laughed, a tinkling sound that conjured images of joyful holiday carolers and left Rosemary no choice but to smile.

Before long, the lights flickered, indicating it was time for the ceremonial portion of the evening to begin. Commissioner Gibson took his place behind the podium that sat atop the stage at the front of the room and began to speak.

"Welcome, everyone, to this year's Fallen Heroes Banquet." He puffed up his chest and went on proudly. "It's unprecedented, but fortunately, we've no men to honor this year. It is not," he paused for dramatic effect, "for lack of a criminal element,"—pause—"but rather due to our commitment to safety, camaraderie, and brotherhood. On those virtues, two men stand out above the rest. Our new chief inspector, Maximilian Whittington, and tonight's honoree, Sergeant Nathaniel Prescott, both overwhelmingly exemplify the values we hold dear."

Rosemary expected the commissioner to elaborate upon Sergeant Prescott's attributes, but it was not to be. Instead, he launched into a touting of the department's accomplishments up to and including a recounting of what seemed like every petty crime that had taken place that year.

"I bet Andrew Lillywhite is rolling over in his grave," Rosemary heard someone say from behind her seat when there was a lull in the commissioner's speech. "Didn't take the old boy long to move in on his best mate's wife."

Her jaw felt like it dropped into her lap, and Max's face contorted into a scowl so fierce it made her heart flutter. He whipped around in his chair the same time she did to see Percy Turner's sardonic smirk pointed towards their table. Three of the men seated at his table guffawed along with him, looking very much like a pack of hyenas and causing Rosemary to wish vehemently that she was a peckish lion.

It only took a few seconds of Max's irate stare to shut the men up, and Percy had the decency to at least appear contrite. Rose recalled the expression on his face when they had pulled up in front of the hall, understanding now why he'd scowled when he noted with whom Max had arrived.

"And now, we'll hear a few words from the man himself, Sergeant Nathaniel Prescott." Commissioner Gibson concluded his speech and returned to the table, unaware of what had transpired in his absence. Judging by the set of Max's jaw, he'd hear about it before the conclusion of the evening.

Nathaniel Prescott stepped onto the stage amid a spattering of applause and flashed a dashing smile in the audience's general direction. It appeared to Rosemary that most of his attention was actually focused on the visage of his wife, who gazed at him with utter devotion.

"Thank you, Commissioner Gibson. While I do appreciate the honor bestowed upon me tonight, I accept it with a heavy heart and also with a caveat. I am no better—take no greater risk—than my fellow officers, nor am I infallible. I've made mistakes I wish I could rectify; I've faced adversity and have fallen in its face as many times as I've risen up before it. Though we celebrate this evening, it is with the knowledge that a killer once again lies in wait somewhere beyond these walls. A killer whose pursuit and capture ranged over several years and cost us a comrade. We have not forgotten the sacrifice of Constable Benton Greene."

As he spoke the words, Prescott locked eyes with a member of the audience seated at a table near the stage.

The object of his gaze, a petite, aging woman with a spattering of freckles across her fair skin, wore a dress of an indeterminate green shade that offset her ginger-colored hair.

"Constable Greene's mother, Mrs. Margot Greene, is in our company tonight. Once again, I'd like to share my sincerest sympathy for the loss of Mrs. Greene's only son. While we have prevented the same from happening to any other officers this year, we must not allow ourselves to become complacent. We must continue to remain vigilant, to expect more from ourselves and each other, and to take responsibility for our actions—and more importantly, for our mistakes."

Ivy leaned over to whisper in Rosemary's ear, "Nate Prescott's been just a doll to Mrs. Greene. She's no family to speak of now, poor dear." It seemed there wasn't a person in the room whose private life was a secret from Ivy Gibson.

Prescott continued, "The city will never be without those who wish to cause harm. As such, our jobs will never be done. I have faith that we will find and apprehend Garrison Black quickly and without further incident. Until then, we can continue to strive for excellence, overcome obstacles, and represent the city of London with both pride and humility. Thank you all."

Sergeant Prescott received a round of applause, marking the end of the ceremonial portion of the evening. Rose's stomach rumbled from a mix of hunger and residual irritation over the remarks Percy Turner had made during the Commissioner's speech. She'd assumed that people would see her with Max and have that sort of contemptuous reaction but had hoped her fears were unfounded. That hadn't proved to be the case, and she supposed she hadn't heard the end of it yet.

Dinner was served almost immediately, and as the plates were placed on the table, Ivy leaned over and reassured Rosemary. "Don't let that cad, Percy, or his cronies ruin your evening," she said, tossing him a glare that he either didn't notice or pretended not to. "He doesn't know the first thing about love, to say nothing about love and loss, and the other three haven't a single lick of sense to share amongst them."

"Thank you," Rose replied sincerely. "I wasn't sure I ought to attend this function at all, but I've discovered that along with Andrew went my concern for the opinions of others. Not that it doesn't chafe hearing the insults, mind you."

Ivy nodded sagely, her shawl slipping from her shoulders to reveal a set of toned arms that belied her advancing years and gave the impression she was the type of woman who didn't actually need a man. Her next admission sealed that supposition. "That's part of the process. I lost two husbands before Alfie, you know," she said in a low voice that only Rose could hear. Not that it mattered, as Commissioner Gibson and Max were engaged in a long-winded discussion about golf, which Rose knew was of little interest to Max considering he couldn't make a putt to save his own life.

"I didn't know that," Rose admitted, wondering if the fact was one of which she should have been aware. "I'm so sorry to learn of your losses."

"It was a long time ago," Ivy waved away Rose's sympathy. "Tragic, of course, but I survived both times. Alfie and I have been married twenty-five years, and we couldn't be happier. He's a stodgy old coot, and I'm two whole handfuls, but we love each other. Suppose I'd continued mourning for the "appropriate" amount of time. In that case, I'd probably be ensconced in some uptown flat with twenty cats by now."

The comment brought a smile to Rosemary's face and calmed her nerves. "It's not as though Max and I are betrothed," she explained, lowering her voice to match Ivy's. "We're just spending some time together and seeing where things go." It was more than she'd usually reveal to a virtual stranger, but Ivy Gibson had a way of making one feel they could speak freely. It was a quality Rosemary appreciated, and she knew somehow that despite Ivy's willingness to gossip, she wouldn't stoop to revealing private comments shared in confidence.

Conversation continued throughout dinner, and all the while, Rosemary noticed that Nathaniel Prescott and his wife barely had a chance to tuck into their meal. People flowed past their table, offering congratulations, and making small talk. Finally, when she suspected their food was stone cold, the pair rose and gathered their things in what appeared an escape attempt.

It was not to be, as Nathaniel Prescott's attention was caught by Mrs. Margot Greene. His wife continued on while he hung back and engaged in a short conversation. Mrs. Greene appeared slightly less entranced by him than Ivy had indicated, allowing him to take her hand, but pulling it away quickly upon release and setting it back in her lap.

Meanwhile, Mrs. Prescott's eyes lit upon Rosemary's table, and she wound her way through the throng to approach the commissioner's wife.

"Hello," Ivy returned Mrs. Prescott's warm greeting and made introductions, which were interrupted by Commissioner Gibson.

"Ivy, it's the Cox couple," he said in what, to him, accounted for a whisper but was clearly heard by half the table. "You simply must provide an excuse to miss their next dinner party. I refuse to eat another meal accompanied by the squawking of that infernal parrot. Your talent for deflection is required. I beg you, come."

With a wry smile and a wink, Ivy left the table to indulge her husband, leaving Rosemary alone with Sergeant Prescott's wife.

Esme Prescott was a slip of a woman with warm blue eyes and dark, almost black hair highlighted with strands of burnished auburn that made her alabaster skin appear almost translucent. Yet, there was nothing particularly special about her, at least from the outside. Obviously, her husband adored her, which in Rosemary's mind meant the special lay underneath. She held out a dainty hand, and Rosemary took it gently, offering her congratulations.

"Mrs. Prescott, you must be terribly proud of your husband," she commented, receiving a wry smile in response.

"Please, call me Esme. And thank you. Of course, I'm quite proud of Nate. The title of Sergeant is an honor he's worked extraordinarily hard to earn." Even to Rosemary, who had just met the woman, the comments sounded rehearsed, giving her the feeling Esme had tired of repeating them. Indeed, she struck Rose as someone who would rather spend her evening next to a roaring fire with a good book than attend a social event of any kind.

Ivy busied herself fawning over her own husband, much to his irritation, and virtually ignored Mrs. Prescott's presence at the table.

"I hear you're quite the lady inspector," Esme said, changing the subject with a twinkle in her eye. "You've solved several murders, isn't that correct?"

Rosemary's cheeks pinked, but she replied with a mixture of pride and modesty that echoed Nathaniel Prescott's earlier sentiment. "The rumors are true. I've been lucky enough to be in the right place at the right time."

"I find it hard to believe it's that simple." It seemed as if Esme might be planning on saying more, but her attention was captured by the strained expression on her husband's face. Indeed, he'd lived to regret his decision to stop and chat.

"Oh, bother. I see poor Nate has been forced into a corner by Margot Greene. I told him he ought not to be so friendly with her, but he never listens. That sounded horrendously insensitive, didn't it?" Rose hardly had a chance to reply before Esme said, "I'd better go save him, or we'll never get out of here. Nice to meet you, Rosemary.

Perhaps I'll see you at another one of these events?"

Rose watched as she sauntered off in the direction of her husband, only to become caught up in conversation at another table before she could make it across the room. Esme's back turned ramrod straight in response to something said by Percy Turner, who had sidled up next to her and was now guffawing at whatever jab he'd taken that had made her bristle.

It took a few more moments for Esme to tear herself away, but she finally did and managed to extricate her husband, mercifully steering Mrs. Greene towards Percy. Rose heard her say, with what she noted was a decidedly evil grin, "Why don't you see to it that Mrs. Greene gets home safely. I'll get her coat."

Esme appeared quite pleased with herself, and the expression on her husband's face was a mixture of relief and appreciation.

He watched his wife's deft handling of both irritations with affection, following her trajectory towards the coat check, his eyes never leaving her back until a figure in lavender satin sidled up next to him.

Something about the timing—combined with the flirtatious jut of the woman's hip—struck Rosemary as far from coincidental, and she didn't realize she was enraptured until she heard another of Ivy's trilling laughs.

"Quite nervy, isn't she?" Ivy said, a bite to her words. "Though not entirely out of the ordinary. Girls do seem to fancy policemen; that's a fact no wife of one could ever deny. Most of the time, it's the kit that does them in. Occasionally a case of what you'd call hero-worship. I'm sure Andrew had at least one in his day." She raised an eyebrow at Rosemary and qualified, "He was quite fetching as well, and such a kind soul."

With a nod, Rosemary allowed that it wasn't outside the realm of possibility but was grateful Andrew had possessed the good sense to keep such details to himself.

"Who is she?" she asked, unable to quell her curiosity.

"That would be Arabelle Grey, heiress," Ivy explained with some disdain. "Her father owned several London hotels, though the poor sod died before he ever had much chance to enjoy his wealth. Arabelle was raised by her aunt and uncle.

Rumor has it she has all the money in the world but can't touch it until she marries. Oh, she gets a hefty allowance, as do her caretakers, but the bulk is tied up with the lawyers. Word is she's broken off at least two engagements. One would think she'd take the first bloke who made an offer. Evidently, she prefers men who are already married."

Somehow, the way Ivy spoke the words that would, on any other person, seem petty managed to come off as merely matter-of-fact. The pair watched as Esme returned from the coat closet and saw Arabelle entertaining her husband. Rosemary's eyes widened as Esme's narrowed, and Ivy chuckled next to her.

"Don't worry about Esme. She can hold her own," Ivy assured just as Arabelle, catching sight of Esme, retreated with a backward, adoring glance at Nathaniel Prescott that made even Rosemary blush.

With a smirk, she noted that the flirtation hadn't gone unnoticed by Percy Turner, either. In fact, he looked as though he wanted to spit nails at Nathaniel Prescott. It was no wonder. Percy's hooked nose and head of disheveled curls were no match for Nate's rugged handsomeness.

Rather than spark a confrontation as Rosemary half expected him to do, Percy steadied himself and ushered Margot Greene out of the building as if she were the third-place prize in the sack race at a village fête.

Chapter Five

It had been a few days since Rose and Vera's unsuccessful dress shopping excursion, and there had been further talk of a quickie wedding ceremony Rosemary knew her mother would be furious over. For once, Vera had given up hope and hadn't even bothered to try tracking down the woman with the perfect gown. Even though it was a long shot to think the owner might be willing to part with such a work of art, Rose knew she would make an attempt if only to mitigate a familial disaster.

And so, with her friend off at yet another play rehearsal, Rosemary went into research mode and finally discovered that the dress had been made for a woman named Betsy Brown who lived on the opposite side of London.

"Wadsworth," Rose shouted, though she needn't have raised her voice; her butler was, as always, waiting nearby in anticipation of his mistress's call. "Would you mind taking me across town? You know how I despise driving on those cobbled streets."

Naturally, he agreed and pulled the car around a short few minutes later. "Where is Miss Vera today?" Wadsworth asked once Rose had explained the reason for the outing.

"Down at the theater, of course, and it's probably a good thing she's not here. If this excursion is a bust, then she doesn't need to know there was ever a glimmer of hope. Trying to talk a woman into giving up her wedding dress, no matter how much I might offer to pay her for it, won't be an easy task."

Shooting Rosemary a grin over his shoulder, Wadsworth assured her, "If anyone possesses the powers of persuasion it will take, it's you, Miss."

Rose smiled. "I can always count on you for a pick-me-up, can't I, Wadsworth? You know, Andrew would be so grateful to see how well you take care of me," she added softly. Wadsworth didn't reply, but his jaw tightened, and he nodded and met her gaze once more before returning his eyes to the road.

When he did speak again, it was after he'd pulled to a stop in front of the address Rosemary had given him, and only to ask, "Shall I come inside with you?"

"No, I don't think that's necessary," Rose replied. She rather thought it would have made things worse, given the destitute nature of the neighborhood. Already she was flaunting her affluence, and the thought made her feel slightly uncomfortable. The notion that she might, under the circumstances, be able to negotiate a sale with the owner of the dress only exacerbated her guilt.

Though she hadn't had any particular expectation of Betsy Brown, Rosemary thought perhaps she'd been given the wrong address when a rather rotund woman in her late twenties answered the door.

Her features—a set of wide green eyes, a pert nose, and full, berry-stained lips—were overshadowed by plump cheeks and a head of flyaway hair that looked as though it hadn't been brushed or styled anytime recently.

She wore a dressing gown that did nothing to hide the bulge around her stomach, and which fell at a mid-calf level and featured a border of fuzzy pom-poms that accentuated the pair of thick ankles sticking out below. The shocking shade of pink made her eyes water.

"Are—are you Betsy Brown?" Rosemary stuttered when the woman stared past her and eyed Wadsworth with suspicion.

"What if I am?" she snapped, pinning Rosemary with a glare.

She thought about turning around and abandoning her mission but knew the disappointment etched across Vera's face would continue to haunt her if she gave up without really trying.

"Was your father a dressmaker at Henninger's bridal shop?" Rose plodded on.

The woman's paper-thin eyebrows shot into her hairline and then crinkled together near the bridge of her nose. She hesitated but then said, "Yes. Why do you want to know?" in a slightly softer tone than her initial inquiry.

Rosemary explained that her friend had seen a photograph of a dress he had made, singing Mr. Brown's praises in hopes of further softening his daughter.

"Come in," Betsy said after a few moments of indecision, leaving the door open and retreating back into the cave-like flat.

With one last glance back at Wadsworth, Rosemary followed, closing the door behind her. If she'd thought Betsy was a character before, her conclusion was confirmed as her eyes scanned the room. It looked like a cross between a shrine and a hovel.

Photographs of younger, considerably svelter Betsy lined the walls; she'd been beautiful not long ago. An aspiring model, judging by the style and quality of the prints.

In one, she wore a scandalously short skirt, one leg kicked back behind her, an impressive amount of cleavage displayed proudly above a midriff-baring top.

But the real kicker was that the mystery of what had happened to the coveted gown was now solved. It hung on a dress form in the center of the sunken living space, the only thing untouched by the detritus lining the rest of the room. Rosemary's heart sank. It was clear to her that talking Betsy into parting with the gown was a fool's errand, and she was beginning to wish she had just let sleeping dogs lie.

A black kitten jumped off the fireplace ledge and landed near Rosemary's feet, causing her to jump and nearly crash into a large glass-shaded lamp. "I'm sorry," she apologized, shooting Betsy a contrite glance and reaching down to pet the cat who had now begun to try to climb her leg.

"Martini!" Betsy shouted, startling Rosemary for the second time in as many minutes. It took her another moment to realize the woman wasn't demanding a drink but was instead admonishing the kitten. "You stop that; you'll ruin the pretty lady's hose." She looked up at one of the photographs and mumbled something about how she'd been a pretty lady once upon a time and then, without another word, disappeared behind a folding screen at the other end of the flat.

Rosemary guessed it was the kitchen area as she heard the sounds of a teakettle being put on to boil and debated making a stealthy exit while Betsy's back was turned. Instead, she steeled herself, perched on the edge of a threadbare sofa, and waited, all the while attempting to curtail the efforts of a purring Martini, who kept trying to shove at Rosemary's face with her nose.

Some minutes later, Betsy emerged with a tray carrying a mismatched tea service. She poured two cups and then loaded a plate with cakes and sandwiches. Through a mouthful of crumbs, she asked, "What business do you have with my father? He's dead, you know." It was said matter-of-factly but carried an undercurrent of pain.

Faltering, Rose tried to figure out how to put her request delicately and finally gave up. "I'd hoped I could convince you to let me buy the gown he made. You see, my friend saw a photograph of the dress, and she fell in love with it. I'd be willing to pay handsomely."

Before she'd even got all the words out, Betsy's chubby face had rearranged into an expression of horror. "Oh, no, I could never part with the dress, not for any amount of money in the world. It's all I have left to remember my Freddie. He died, too." She looked longingly at the gown before returning her gaze to Rosemary, her eyes filling with unshed tears.

"I'm very sorry to hear that," Rosemary replied quietly. "Coincidentally, the man my friend is marrying happens to be named Fred as well—and he's also my brother. Why don't you tell me about your Freddie," she prompted.

Betsy swallowed her last bite of cake and set the empty plate down on the tea tray. Her eyes misted again, and she stared straight ahead, avoiding Rosemary's gaze while she spoke. "He was the most wonderful man, a pilot in the war. So handsome, so virile—my father thought him vain, but there's a difference between confidence and brashness." Her voice slurred slightly, and Rosemary eyed the woman's teacup while wondering if she had a flask hidden somewhere in the sofa cushions.

Martini had finished searching the floor for errant crumbs and, finding her owner had left her none, returned to Rosemary's side to continue vying for attention. As she gave in and scratched behind the kitten's ears, Rosemary recalled Ivy Gibson's comment from the prior evening regarding ending up an old spinster cat lady. All Betsy needed was a few more furry companions, and she'd match that description word for word.

"Freddie could accomplish anything he put his mind to, and what he wanted was to fly," Betsy had continued while Rosemary's inner thoughts went down another path. "He said he felt like his rig was an extension of himself. As though he grew wings the moment he entered the cockpit. I suppose it must have felt like a betrayal when the engines failed, and he went down along with his beloved plane. I've wondered about that so many times. What must have flashed through his mind while he was spiraling out of control? Did he think of me then, in those last moments? It haunts you, you know."

She shivered, and her eyes flicked to Rosemary's for a fraction of a second. "I wasn't even allowed to attend the funeral—if there was one at all. It was as though when Freddie died, his mother and father couldn't stand the pain of it. They cut all ties with me, and I don't even know where he's buried."

Betsy's story tripped off her tongue in such a rehearsed way that Rosemary suspected she'd repeated those words over and over—likely to nobody but herself, given the solitary existence the woman seemed to lead.

Still, Rose was forced to swallow the lump of sympathy that had formed in her throat. "That must have been—must be—very difficult for you," she said sincerely, unable to imagine herself in Betsy's shoes. It was one thing to lose a lover; quite another to have been given no opportunity to say a final goodbye or a place to honor his memory. "I lost my other brother, Lionel, in the war. I still remember the day we heard the news. I'll never forget it as long as I live."

"All I have is the telegram I received, saying he was gone." Betsy pulled a piece of tattered paper from her pocket and handed it to Rosemary. She glanced at the words on the paper but could not give it back to Betsy, whose hands had already gone back to shoveling bites of sandwiches into her mouth. "I still walk our special path through the park every day," she said wistfully after swallowing. "We would search the trees and benches for knots that looked like hearts. He'd always say they were put there special, just for us. Sometimes I fancy I'll find him sitting there, waiting for me, but I never do."

"My friend, the one who is marrying my brother Freddie, was first engaged to my late brother, Lionel," Rosemary said, thinking perhaps the commonality between Vera and Betsy might soften the woman towards the idea of giving up the gown.

"It took her years to get over it, and eventually, she realized that Frederick was the only man on earth who could fill Lionel's shoes. She's finally happy, and what would send her over the moon would be the chance to wear the perfect dress for her wedding."

Betsy's eyes had narrowed to slits. "She must not really have loved Lionel then," she said. "If she was able to cast his memory aside in favor of another man." The idea riled Betsy, who made a move to stand.

As she rose from her seat, little Martini launched herself from Rosemary's lap and caught one of the pom-poms from Betsy's dressing gown in her claws. Betsy teetered on one foot, let out a booming expletive, and began to topple in the direction of the sofa.

Rosemary hastily tucked the telegram into her own dress pocket as she tried to keep Betsy from hurting herself on the way down, but the woman landed in a heap on the sofa, completely unharmed.

"Well," Rose said ruefully, "if I ever thought I might like a kitten, your little Martini here has just cured me of it. Not that she isn't adorable."

"She's a pest," Betsy said as she rearranged herself and reached for the last cake on the plate. "However, beggars can't be choosers, and she's good company. What was it you wanted again?" she asked foggily, cinching Rosemary's suspicion that perhaps there was a little something extra in Betsy's teacup.

It took another forty-five minutes for Rosemary to make her escape, and in that span, she heard the story of Betsy's Freddie twice more, with little variation. She'd been shown a faded photograph of a handsome man—Betsy hadn't exaggerated there—and watched as another plate of cakes disappeared down the poor, depressed woman's gullet.

By the time she made it back to the car, Rosemary felt as though her own stomach were full to bursting.

"Wadsworth, get me out of here, immediately!" she said, hurrying to the car before she could be called back inside for another round.

It wasn't until Rosemary was halfway home that she realized Betsy's prized telegram was still in her pocket. "Oh, lordy, I'm going to have to go back," she said aloud.

Wadsworth immediately slowed the car down and took a right-hand turn. "Not now," Rosemary clarified. "It will have to be another day. I don't think I can take any more. Perhaps I'll just put this telegram in an envelope and send it back to her."

"I'll take care of it if you'd like," he replied, reaching for the paper. Rosemary made a move to hand it to him and then thought better of it.

"No, it's all right. I'll handle it. Thank you," she said, stuffing the slip of paper in her pocket and laying back against the seat with her eyes closed. It was going to be a long time before she could look at another petit four without thinking of Betsy Brown's shapeless dressing gown.

CHAPTER SIX

Rosemary didn't sleep well that night. She couldn't stop dreaming about Betsy Brown and her poor, dead Freddie. Warplanes falling out of the sky swirled into a dingy flat with trays of cakes on all the tables and a dozen kittens mewing loudly. One of them yawled, and she woke with a start. That's why, nearly an hour earlier than usual, she had made her way down to the dining room in search of a hot cup of tea.

Instead of something to quench her thirst, Rose was treated to a screech coming from the kitchen and overheard the cook, Helen, berating Wadsworth.

"That man has called here at least ten times in the last three days looking for you. I've still got to cover for Mrs. Moore, you know. Can't be your answering service as well, now can I?"

Patiently—more patiently than Rosemary herself would have been able to remain—he replied, "I don't understand—never mind. I do apologize for the inconvenience, Helen. You can tell him I'm simply not available."

"If he rings one more time, you'll take it. I've got too much work to do and no time for nonsense," Helen spat, her mouth dropping open mid-sentence as she emerged from the kitchen and realized her mistress was seated at the dining room table.

Rosemary raised an eyebrow, causing the cook's cheeks to further redden. "Apologies, Miss Rose. I didn't realize you were awake. I'll just go get your tea."

"Yes, please do," she said, watching Helen's shoulders slump as she turned and bustled back out.

"Now, whatever is the problem?" Rose asked Wadsworth once the cantankerous Helen was out of earshot. "It can't simply be the cutlery faux pas unless Helen has become completely unhinged."

Wadsworth's jaw clenched, and he avoided her gaze but could not bring himself to ignore her completely. "It's a personal matter," was all he would say.

Just as Rosemary opened her mouth to coax more information from her butler, the telephone trilled out another high-pitched ring, eliciting an irritated grunt from the direction of the kitchen.

"Wadsworth, there's a call for you," Helen said, returning to the dining room with a tea tray in her hands. "Please make it stop," she begged with an obvious effort to keep her voice from returning to its former, hysterical tone.

He bowed his head and acquiesced, leaving the room without a word. Helen muttered in German, "Du hast die Manieren eines Schweins," unaware that Rosemary understood every word.

"Das reicht völlig," Rosemary deadpanned.

Helen's head jerked to look at her mistress, her cheeks flaming pink. "Apologies, Miss Rose. I'm out of sorts today, is all." She tried to brush the incident aside, and Rosemary allowed her to do so, her point having been made.

When Wadsworth returned from the parlor, his face was pale, and his expression grim.

"Is everything all right?" Rose asked, her brow wrinkling.

"I suspect so. However, it seems there is a problem I must address immediately," he replied. "Will you be able to get by without me for the morning?"

"Assuredly. After all, Helen is here," Rose said loudly, a twinkle in her eye, as the cook made her way back into the dining room. "She's perfectly capable of handling the household while you're out. Take all the time you need."

The volume of Helen's footsteps increased to a near stomp as she traversed the kitchen, and she spoke nary another word to Rosemary throughout the rest of breakfast. It was just as well, Rosemary thought, content to avoid a confrontation for the time being.

Instead, she descended the stairs to the lowest level of the townhouse, donned a paint smock to protect her dress, and went about the task of readying her palette in the hopes of finishing a painting she'd begun earlier in the week.

After an hour or so of trying to effectively translate the image in her mind's eye to the canvas before her, Rosemary finally gave up and swapped it out for a fresh one.

Thoughts of her adventure the previous day had persisted to the point of obsession, and it was there that Vera found her some time later.

"Who's that handsome fellow?" she asked, hanging her handbag and coat on a rack near the door. She rested a hand on her friend's shoulder, coming away with a smear of red paint splashed across her fingers. "Another one of London's finest boys in blue?"

Rosemary stepped back to appraise her work and explained, "No, that's Freddie," she said, receiving a puzzled glance in response. "He was a pilot who perished in the war, and his fiancée is the owner of the fabulous wedding dress you've been pining after."

"What did you do, Rosie?" The hint of hope in Vera's voice was unmistakable.

With a sigh, Rose was forced to reply, "Nothing. At least, nothing yet. You wouldn't have believed it, Vera. The woman is stuck so firmly in the past that she's barely living. It's quite sad, and

I'd like to believe there's a way to bring her a measure of comfort, but I can't begin to figure how."

She explained how Betsy hadn't been allowed to attend Freddie's funeral and how she didn't even know where her betrothed was buried. "I think if she could visit his gravesite, she'd be able to start moving on."

"I can't believe you went to see her without me," Vera sulked, her eyes narrowed to slits.

Rosemary rolled her own, and when she spoke again, it was as though she were talking to a child. "You didn't miss much, and since I'll be needing to return the telegram I accidentally swiped, I'm sure you'll get your chance to gawk at the woman."

Somewhat mollified, Vera took a seat behind Rosemary, checking first to ensure no more of her would get coated in paint, and stared at the painting. "I can see why she's gone to ground. If I'd lost a man like that, I would probably turn into a hermit too."

"That's not true," Rosemary said, her tone gentler now. "You did lose a man like that. We both did, and yet here we are, going on with our lives. It's indulgent to simply turn one's back on everything and everyone. Perhaps Betsy doesn't have anyone left to care about her, and that's the difference between us."

Vera thought about it for a moment while Rosemary continued her work, adding a few highlights to Freddie's neck and cheeks. "That's quite sad, isn't it?"

"I suppose so," Rose replied, her eyes still trained on the canvas.

"I'd have thought you'd have more sympathy for her position," Vera retorted.

Rose sighed and turned to her friend. "I do have sympathy for her loss. However, I find myself mildly irritated by the way she decided to handle her grief."

"Not everyone is quite as stoic as you'd like them to be, Rosie." Vera didn't add that she could vividly remember her friend having dissolved into a veritable puddle of grief. It had taken months of cajoling from her and Frederick before Rose returned to herself. Recognizing that it typically worked the other way around—Rosemary taking care of others—she decided not to press the subject and allowed her friend to work through whatever emotions Betsy Brown's plight had raised.

Instead, she got to her feet and tugged on Rosemary's arm. "Let's go have a cup of tea, and you can tell me all the sordid details. Where is Wadsworth, anyway? He didn't greet me at the door."

"He's attending to a personal matter," Rose explained, then glanced up at the clock mounted above the door. Her brow furrowed, and she divested herself of paints and smock. "He ought to have been back long before now. Perhaps Helen resumed berating him for his perceived crimes; in which case, he'll need our help escaping her clutches."

But when she and Vera ascended the stairs to the townhouse proper, the butler was still nowhere to be found. They wandered into the dining room, finding Frederick sitting in front of an empty place setting and scowling. "Whatever is the matter with your staff, Rosie?" he demanded.

Rosemary ignored him, save for an irritated glare, and finally entered the kitchen where Helen stood over a hot hob, also glaring into a pot of bubbling stew.

"Has Wadsworth returned?" Rose earned herself a glare that bordered on being disrespectful.

"No, madam, not as yet," Helen replied tersely, pressing her lips together with effort.

Just then, the sound of the front door opening echoed through the house, followed by heavy footsteps thudding across the floor. Rose and Vera shared a sense of relief and scurried back out of the kitchen and away from Helen's scowl.

Except it wasn't Wadsworth returning home, it was Max and the look on his face—combined with the fact he'd simply walked into the house without knocking—made Rose tremble.

He was out of breath as if he'd been running again, and when he gazed into her eyes, she could see pain etched in his.

"It's Wadsworth," Max said, his voice breaking. "He's been arrested for murder."

Chapter Seven

The blood drained from Rosemary's face while she processed Max's declaration. "What?" She assessed the wobble in her knees, decided they would hold her, but her hands shook, and her voice turned shrill. "What do you mean, *arrested for murder*? Whose murder? Wadsworth wouldn't hurt a fly, and you know it. Not unless he was defending himself."

Vera's eyes were wide, and the dumbfounded expression on Frederick's face said more than words could have conveyed.

"I know, Rose," Max said, holding up his hands in intense frustration, "but it's more complicated than that. You see, Wadsworth was caught, quite literally red-handed, standing over the body. Not only that, but the dead man is Nathaniel

Prescott." The statement fell like a stone, followed by a moment of complete silence.

Rose turned even paler and grimaced, thinking first of Esme Prescott, whose life would never be the same again, and then of Wadsworth, who had been by her side during the same difficult time in her life. Unable to wrap her head around Max's words, she pressed her fingers to her temples and took a deep breath.

The sound of banging pots echoed from the kitchen, and Rosemary directed the group into the parlor, citing a need for privacy. Helen didn't need any more ammunition when it came to her hatred for Wadsworth, and if one more tart remark popped out of the cook's mouth, Rose feared Max would be forced to take her into custody along with her butler.

There, she found Anna standing on a chair with a feather duster in her hand, attempting to rid the bric-a-brac lining the upper shelves of a thick layer of dust that had accumulated in Mrs. Moore's absence.

"Come down from there," she commanded softly, then poured herself a glass of brandy and explained the situation to a stunned Anna.

The girl let out a squeak, her response much the same as Rosemary's had been, and breathed, "No, not Wadsworth. It can't be."

"No, it can't be," Rosemary agreed, downing the brandy and beginning to pace about the room. She'd declined to offer a drink to anyone else, deciding the lot of them could fend for themselves, which Frederick did even while he fumed.

"You can't possibly believe my doting butler would murder a police officer?" This she directed at Max, who sighed and slumped into an armchair.

He half expected Wadsworth to step in and hand him the strong drink he so desperately needed at that moment, shaking his head at the irony of the situation. "I'm not telling you I think he did anything. Even if it wasn't Wadsworth we're talking about, I stand for the belief that one is innocent until proved guilty. Not to mention the fact there are too many inconsistencies for me to believe the accusation will stick."

It took Rose a few more seconds to process what she was being told, but in the meantime, Frederick stepped in and made the demand she didn't have breath to speak. "What sort of inconsistencies?"

"Well," Max explained, "for one thing, Nate was shot in the heart with a revolver, which so far hasn't been found at the scene. The time it would have taken for him to bleed to death from a wound like that wouldn't have given Wadsworth enough time to hide the murder weapon. Furthermore, the maid says Prescott had several visitors this morning yet can't confirm who arrived or at what time.

Unfortunately, the rest of the staff had the day off, and Mrs. Prescott was out shopping. Regardless, Wadsworth was on the scene, covered in blood. That's still enough for an arrest, whether I believe he was responsible or not. Which, of course, I don't." Max reiterated, his tone somewhat defensive, and understandably so considering the backlash from Rosemary when he'd been forced to investigate Freddie for a crime he also hadn't committed just a few months prior.

"I've made sure he's comfortable, and I've asked my best men—men I'm certain I can trust—to keep an eye on him," Max assured.

Rosemary heaved a sigh of relief. "That's not enough to get him hanged. As soon as the commissioner realizes that, he ought to release Wadsworth, oughtn't he?"

Again, Max appeared doubtful, causing Rose's spirits to plunge even further. "I certainly hope so, but the department is in a state of flux at the moment. We just finished celebrating the fact that no officers have perished in the line of duty this year, yet there's an escaped mass murderer on the loose, and now a cop has been murdered in what appears to be cold blood."

"Was not Sergeant Prescott the man responsible for putting said mass murderer behind bars in the first place? A mass murderer who habitually shoots his victims in the heart? Isn't it far more probable that *he's* the one responsible for the murder?" Rosemary demanded. "Why isn't Commissioner Gibson increasing the search for Garrison Black? He already killed one constable; doesn't it stand to reason he could have killed another?"

"It does," Max assured, and then dashed Rosemary's hopes with his next statement, "and it doesn't. Most gunshot wounds intended to kill are aimed at the chest or head. It doesn't implicate Black any more than it does anyone else. However, combined with the fact Black had an obvious vendetta against the man who'd been chasing him for ten years does make a difference. In fact, that's exactly what I pointed out to the commissioner. I know it's small comfort, but I don't think he really believes Wadsworth is the killer, either. What I do know is that he's taking a lot of heat right now, and we needed to make an arrest."

Max declined to elaborate on that point, and Rosemary could feel her hackles rise. "When you say *we* do you actually mean *you*? Was it you who made the arrest?"

"I had no choice, Rose, honestly. The order came down from the commissioner himself. Just think what it would do to the city of London if the public thought Garrison Black was even more dangerous than they already believe. Keeping Wadsworth in custody makes it appear as though we're on top of things and takes the focus off the investigation into Black's escape."

"So it's all political," Frederick nearly shouted, slamming his own freshly-poured bourbon down onto one of Rosemary's favorite end tables. The liquid sloshed onto its surface, and even though she knew it would ruin the veneer, she couldn't bring herself to either care or admonish her brother. "An innocent man rotting in jail to cover up the fact that the police allowed a convict to escape? That's ludicrous," he boomed, receiving a chagrined look from Max. "You're the chief inspector. Don't you have any pull?"

"I am," Max said slowly, "But there's still a chain of command, and I'm nowhere near the top. I know it doesn't seem fair, and it's not. I'm looking into it, rest assured." Max explained.

"Shush, Freddie," Rosemary urged. "I suppose you've no promising leads on Black's whereabouts?" This she directed at Max.

"Not as yet," he admitted slowly, avoiding her gaze.

She jammed her empty hand onto her hip and raised one eyebrow. "What aren't you telling us?"

"I'm telling you everything I can tell you, Rose, and leaving out only what I'm obligated to under my oath as an officer. I've said too much already." He knew his words would have little effect on her; her tenacity was one of the things he admired most about Rosemary, though at times like this, it seemed a curse rather than a blessing. She stared him down until his resolve cracked, and he caved in to her demand.

"We believe Black's escape wasn't entirely his doing. The department has nearly eradicated the...let's just say *unsavory element* that's been present in the district since the war."

"Explain, please," Rosemary demanded.

"One concern has been the employment of brutality to elicit confessions from suspects or testimony from witnesses. Another was the discovery of two cases," Max blushed, but didn't allow his gaze to waver, "of sexual impropriety."

Rosemary found the revelation shocking, but there was more to come.

"Corruption in any part of an organization becomes a stain on the rest. Any officer who accepts a bribe is no better than the criminal who offers it." His voice rose in volume to enforce the statement.

"I had no idea," Rosemary said. "How positively galling."

"Yes, indeed," Max agreed. "We've routed out most of the problem; thought we'd got the last of it when the chief inspector before me was ousted—you remember Chief Inspector Crowley— but once a boil appears, it will always fester. Every so often, key evidence goes missing, or a witness changes their testimony at the last minute and sinks our chances of a conviction. The commissioner feels, and I agree that the problem in our ranks is still present."

Rose nodded. "It seems likely."

"As you can imagine, this situation is a bureaucratic nightmare. I'm up against a wall, Rose, and my tenure as chief inspector has barely begun. To say I need to tread carefully is an understatement. I can't tell you any more right now, but this goes deeper than Andy and I thought."

Rosemary started at the mention of Andrew. It wasn't often that his name escaped Max's lips; out of nothing more than his own grief over the loss of a trusted friend, Rose had surmised, but still, it struck her odd that Max would bring him up at this juncture.

"What does Andrew have to do with any of this?" she demanded, her voice coming out at a slightly higher pitch than she'd intended.

"Nothing," Max said quickly, "except for the fact that this sort of thing is exactly what he abhorred. Corruption within the unit hurts everyone in the unit—and most especially, the good cops. That's what Andy used to say."

Rose stopped mid-pace and strode towards the door. "I want to see Wadsworth, and I'd like to have a word with the commissioner. Perhaps I can persuade him—" she stopped short at the look on Max's face. "What?"

"It won't help, I'm afraid. I've already appealed to Commissioner Gibson, and he has no intention of sticking his neck out until there's something solid to go on."

"Fine," Rosemary replied petulantly, the idea of forcing the commissioner to see her already solidifying with intention she was content to hide from Max. "He can't stop me from visiting Wadsworth, can he?"

Max winced and looked as though he'd like to jump out the window rather than say whatever came next. "The commissioner can't, no, but Wadsworth made it very clear to me that you are not to be admitted into the jailhouse. He made me swear an oath."

Vera swore an oath, but not the kind Max meant. He spared her a glance but wisely refrained from commenting when she called Wadsworth's character and parentage into question with a series of words most women would consider unfitting. Judging by the look she directed at him, Max wondered if Vera might be thinking up a few epithets to direct his way as well.

Rosemary refilled her brandy and downed the contents in one gulp, contemplating throwing the glass into the fireplace when she was through. In her wildest flights of fancy, she couldn't conceive of a set of circumstances where Wadsworth might commit murder. The only way to parse out a possible motive was to talk to the man, and he'd made that impossible. If the slightest trace of doubt regarding his innocence crossed her mind, she tamped it down. Wadsworth wouldn't kill in cold blood.

"It's not hopeless. I still have interviews to conduct with Prescott's staff, and my men are keeping the scene secured until I return. Wadsworth wasn't the only person to visit Nate that day. We know that for certain; however, if I were a betting man, I'd place my money on Garrison Black. He's dangerous, deranged, and incensed at having been caught in the first place. He hated Nate. So much so that I'm not surprised he broke his previous pattern. That alone speaks volumes regarding his state of mind. Black's emotions may just be his demise. One can hope."

Sulkily, Rosemary peered at Max through narrowed eyes. "There has to be something I can do to help," she insisted.

"Not when it comes to Black, there's not," he retorted quickly, worry evident in his tone. "He's desperate, and I don't want you involving yourself with a convicted mass murderer, particularly one who's more deranged than ever. Am I understood?"

This time, Max's tone brooked no refusal, and Rosemary wouldn't have argued the point anyway. She was smarter than that and told him so in no uncertain terms.

"I won't lie down and allow Wadsworth to be hanged for a murder he didn't commit, but I'll keep out of the Black situation, on one condition."

"What condition is that?" Max asked, feeling his heart sink.

Rosemary looked him dead in the eyes and replied, "That you tell me whatever else it is that you're not saying. I know there's more." She crossed her arms and waited.

"Good one, Rosie," Vera encouraged.

Lying to her would certainly save her from fretting, but it wasn't just the case or Wadsworth's life on the line, Max decided. His relationship with Rosemary was also at stake, and that was more important than all the rest. Furthermore, given her propensity for investigation, she would ferret out what he'd held back until now. It would, he thought, be better if he were the one to explain.

"There is one more thing, but telling you not only breaks a promise I made to Wadsworth but one I made to Andy. There's another reason why Commissioner Gibson isn't willing to drop the charges against Wadsworth."

"Well, what is it, man?" Frederick demanded. "Out with it already."

Max ran his fingers through his hair and grimaced, then dropped a bomb. "Before he became your butler, Carrington Wadsworth was Andrew's partner. He was Sergeant Wadsworth back then."

The admission forced Rosemary into a seat, and she thought the glass in her hand might now shatter as she clutched it so tightly her knuckles turned white. Her mouth opened and closed without sound as she found herself speechless once again.

Thoughts and memories raced through her mind, the pieces of a puzzle she hadn't known existed falling into place. She understood now why Andrew had treated Wadsworth the way he had, why he'd trusted him with his and her life, and why Wadsworth had stayed so loyal and protective after Andrew's death. What she didn't understand was why Wadsworth had decided to go from a police sergeant to a butler and why he'd left police work in the first place.

Max must know the answers to at least one of those questions, Rosemary thought, though when she inquired as to the reason for Wadsworth's departure, he insisted he had no more time for questions and took his leave.

Once he'd gone, Vera indulged herself in another spate of offensive language before enfolding Rosemary in a comforting embrace. "We'll sort this out and have Wadsworth back in no time. You just wait and see."

CHAPTER EIGHT

For several days, Nathaniel Prescott's murder and Wadsworth's subsequent arrest made the front page news right alongside the number one story of escaped mass murderer Garrison Black. Even though Rosemary was certain the two crimes were connected, they shared nothing but a margin.

Local hero slain! Former officer caught red-handed! Inquest to be held this afternoon. read the headline, followed by a quote from Commissioner Alfie Gibson, who stated that "Justice will surely be served!" Rose could imagine him thrusting his fist in the air as he spoke the words, and it made her want to spit nails.

Tears welling in her wide green eyes, Anna read the story over Rosemary's shoulder. "It's a right mess. You'd only have to meet him to know our Wadsworth would never do for a man that way. What is the world coming to?"

"I don't have the foggiest idea," Rosemary agreed, patting Anna on her hand. Something about the tone and cadence of her voice struck Rosemary as unfamiliar.

Anna had worked as her personal maid for near on two years now. She'd been but a girl when she started, just out of school and fearful for her future. It was a wonder Anna hadn't married right off; she'd a good head on her pretty little shoulders, but Rosemary suspected she had her sights set on something other than domestic life. Now, though, Anna sounded like a woman, slightly older and somewhat more jaded than she'd been when she started.

A stab of guilt pierced Rosemary's heart. Poor Anna had become embroiled in more than one murder investigation during her tenure as maid, and it seemed as though the experience had taken its toll. Perhaps the girl could use some time off. When all this was over, she'd send Anna on a lovely little holiday and hope the girl didn't decide never to return to London at all!

Rosemary shook her head to rid it of the notion and brought her attention back to the present. The day of the inquest had come—pushed through extraordinarily quickly despite Max's assurances that the department wasn't rushing as speedily to judgment as the papers would indicate—and Rosemary was beside herself.

She'd do anything to help Wadsworth out of the mess he was in, desperately wanting him back home where he belonged. She had spent the evening prior peppering Max with questions during the brief interlude he'd had between shifts, and he wasn't pleased about it. She felt the same about his lack of new information and was now even more worried about Wadsworth's fate.

Rosemary's resolve solidified further when Helen whipped open the kitchen door and stalked to the table with the breakfast dishes. She set them down with a clatter and heaved off again, stopping short when she noticed the paper lying next to Rosemary's place setting.

"Looks like old Waddy got his revenge for whatever it was that man did to him, don't it?" Helen commented so snidely Rose dropped the scone she'd been preparing to slather with soft butter. "He'll be hanged, he will, I'd wager my next month's pay on it."

"Enough, Helen. I'm perfectly aware of your opinion regarding Wadsworth, but I must put my foot down. Baseless accusations have no place in this house. Unless you know something I don't—" at this, Helen shook her head reluctantly— "We stand together or not at all, is that clear?"

Rosemary realized she sounded exactly like her overbearing mother, whose staff tended to run scared whenever she walked through a door. Yet, she took a small amount of pleasure in the expression on Helen's face and decided that in some instances, perhaps Evelyn had the right idea. She knew for sure none of the staff at Woolridge House would dare speak one word against another in front of her mother.

Helen stomped into the kitchen without further comment, allowing the door to slam behind her as though it might count as getting the last word. Rose put the scone back on its tray, her appetite having flown, and headed upstairs to her room to dress for the inquest.

Upon her arrival at the courthouse, flanked by Frederick and Vera, Rosemary spotted Esme

Prescott sitting in the front row and dabbing her eyes with a handkerchief. She looked every bit the grieving widow, and once again, Rosemary's heart constricted, forcing her to stop in her tracks and clutch Vera's hand to steady herself. After a moment, she felt another presence appear beside her and looked up into Max's face.

Stoic as always, he said nothing but took her other hand in his and led the threesome down the aisle towards a set of seats positioned directly behind Esme. Rosemary hesitated and whispered to Max, "Maybe we should sit in the back. I'm not entirely certain Esme Prescott will welcome me here, given the police have arrested my butler for her husband's murder."

"You've a right to be here, Rose," he replied. "And if anyone gives you any trouble—"

"They won't," Frederick interjected, "Or they'll have to deal with Vera and me." Of the two, Vera would be the more formidable opponent.

Max's lip quirked, but his expression quickly reverted to its former state of furrowed brow and dark, brooding eyes. He took a seat next to Rosemary and clasped her hand in his. Esme stared across the courtroom, her eyes following the figure of Arabelle Grey, who had taken a seat in the opposite aisle next to Margot Greene.

Rosemary swallowed a nervous giggle when she noted that both women had once again dressed in homage to their individual monikers; Arabelle in a grey sheath and Margot swathed in a moss-colored number that reminded her of something found in a baby's nappy. Upon further inspection, she realized the two had not arrived together, nor did they exchange any pleasantries.

Arabelle stared straight ahead, her eyes rimmed with red as though she were the one who'd been widowed, and didn't appear to notice the daggers Esme stared in her direction. Meanwhile, Margot's eyes were locked on Esme's hunched figure, a look of sympathy etched across her face.

A few moments passed before Esme noticed who'd taken the seat behind her. Rosemary's heart skipped a beat as the woman's eyes met hers. When treated to a thin-lipped, grim smile of what appeared to be welcome, Rosemary was surprised—shocked, even—at the lack of anger or malice.

How very odd, Rosemary thought, after Esme had turned back around, and her heartbeat returned to normal. She vowed to speak to Esme after the proceedings were over, but that was the last thought she had because just then, Wadsworth was led into the courtroom.

She had never before seen him wearing anything other than his butler's kit, but now he had on that of a prisoner. Even though he held his head high and his shoulders squared, he still looked somehow smaller than ever before.

When his eyes locked with Rosemary's, she nearly burst into tears. Even though it vexed her greatly that he refused to admit her to visit him, she reminded herself that what he needed now was support, and so she put on a stiff upper lip and gave him an encouraging smile. He returned it with the same amount of fondness as usual, which wrenched her heart even more.

Vera stiffened beside her, and Frederick let out a hiss. Wadsworth avoided looking directly at either of them, as though he'd spent all his energy on Rosemary and had none left save for what he needed to make it through the proceedings.

A hush fell over the room as the coroner, a short man with a somewhat florid complexion and a nervous habit of clearing his throat, approached the podium and described, in great detail, the cause of Sergeant Nathaniel Prescott's death. He'd been shot in the chest with a .455 round, most likely from a Webley service revolver. Death occurred within ten minutes.

Next, each of the involved parties was called forward to present their evidence.

"First, we'll hear from Chief Inspector Maximilian Whittington."

Max described the scene with which he was met upon his arrival at the Prescott residence that day.

"I arrived at the victim's home at approximately 3:15pm. When I entered the study, I recognized Mr. Carrington Wadsworth, former sergeant, kneeling over the body with his hands on Sergeant Prescott's chest."

Rosemary gulped at the vivid image rising in her imagination.

Max continued, "Mr. Wadsworth shouted to me that Sergeant Prescott had been shot and that he was trying to stop the bleeding. I rushed forward to help, but it was too late. Sergeant Prescott took his last breath moments after I arrived."

Esme sat silent while she listened to the accounting, the occasional quiver of her shoulders the only sign of her distress.

"I then interviewed Mr. Wadsworth, who explained that he had found Sergeant Prescott unconscious and suffering from a bullet wound to the chest." Max spared a glance in his direction and said, "When asked, Mr. Wadsworth stated he had come to visit the deceased at his request and seemed quite shaken by the experience. He made no attempt to flee and offered any and all assistance without hesitation. "

When Max was asked whether he'd been summoned to the Prescott residence, he replied, "No, as it happens, I'd received a request from Sergeant Prescott, asking if I might stop by to pick up some important case files and deliver them to the office at the start of my shift. As such, I arrived mere moments before Sergeant Prescott's death. A search did not reveal the murder weapon on or near Mr. Wadsworth or even in the vicinity of the body. It is unlikely, in my opinion, that Mr. Wadsworth would have had sufficient time to hide the gun if he were the murderer. My personal suspicion is the killer escaped through the direct exit from Sergeant Prescott's study into the private, fenced-in side garden, and from there simply walked out the gate without being seen."

Rosemary noted that despite Max's statement, Arabelle Grey glared at Wadsworth with an expression of hatred. As she looked around, the sentiment seemed to echo across the faces of much of the crowd.

Most of the officers in attendance—several constables, and of course Commissioner Gibson, who sat at the end of Esme Prescott's row— attempted to appear impartial. Some even nodded at Wadsworth in encouragement, but a few were unable to hide their contempt. For example, Constable Percy Turner's face had twisted into a contemptuous sneer that had Rosemary's blood boiling.

The implications setting in, her heart sank, and she was forced to bite back a sob. Nothing that Max said was news to her, as she'd sufficiently grilled him the evening prior. She forced herself to tamp down her feelings and instead turned her attention to the next witness called to testify: the accused himself.

Wadsworth spoke clearly, his voice strong and confident despite what must have been an incredible toll.

"Unfortunately, I can't say why Sergeant Prescott wanted to meet with me on the day of his death. He rang me several times over the last two weeks, and I had declined to speak to him or reply to his messages."

Rosemary could attest to that. She tried to catch Wadsworth's eye, but he refused to so much as glance in her direction.

"We worked together for roughly eighteen months prior to my departure from the police department, and I was reluctant to revisit that time in my life. When Sergeant Prescott persisted, I did agree to meet him at his home, which I had not previously visited."

Now, Wadsworth looked right at Rosemary. She'd have believed his statement in any case, but his direct gaze cemented her faith in his veracity.

"When I arrived, the front door stood open, and the scent of cordite filled the air. I called out to the residents of the home, receiving no answer before entering. Still calling out to the family, I made my way inside, checking each room as I went. I found Sergeant Prescott in his study, still alive but bleeding profusely from a bullet wound to the chest. I rushed to his aid, pressing my hands to the wound in an attempt to stop the bleeding."

Wadsworth's voice broke slightly, and he looked down at his hands as if remembering the blood that had stained them. A moment passed while he composed himself.

"I can't say how much time passed before Chief Inspector Whittington arrived, but it couldn't have been more than a minute or two. When it was clear that Mr. Prescott was deceased, Inspector Whittington asked for my statement, which I gave. At that time, he informed me that under the circumstances, I would likely be detained. For the record, I considered Sergeant Prescott a friend—an estranged friend, yes—but a friend nonetheless."

His statement was followed by some tittering from the crowd, but there was no denying that Wadsworth and Max's stories perfectly aligned. Still, Rosemary knew facts didn't always matter when it came to the collective opinion—and the collective opinion seemed to be that Wadsworth was guilty of murder.

Oh, they'd figure out a way to reconcile Max's statement with their preconceived notions, helped along, no doubt, by headlines designed to keep the paperboys on their toes. Rosemary had to tamp down her disgust as Esme took her turn on the stand.

"I don't have much to say," the widow declared. "I was not at home that day. I was out shopping." Esme paused here, her eyes welling with unshed tears. Something about her delivery of the statement struck Rosemary as odd, but then she remembered the day Andrew had died. If she had been out, doing something as frivolous as shopping, she probably never would have forgiven herself.

"Nate told me he'd appointments to keep that morning and to take my time. He didn't say with whom, only that they were work-related, and I didn't pry." She appeared to have reached her limit and was mercifully allowed to step down.

Mrs. Patricia Pratt, the Prescott family's maid—a timid-looking matronly sort with bottle-bottom glasses—took the stand next. After much hemming and hawing, she finally began, "If I'd only known...I would never have—," she dithered in that manner for some few moments before being prodded to speak plainly.

"The doorbell rang at least three times that morning. I was in a right state. It was my day to polish the silver. Master Prescott said he would be in his study, and as he was expecting callers, he would listen for the front door." Finally, she managed a coherent thought.

She tilted her head sideways as if dredging up a memory. "The tea service took an absolute age, don't you know." She began to list the pieces she'd done, and it took a stern word to bring her back to the matter at hand.

"I'd only begun working on the teaspoons when the master asked if I might just nip down to the tobacconist for a pack of Woodbines. Nasty smelling things, you ask me."

No one had. Mrs. Pratt described her dismay upon returning to find Inspector Whittington as the bearer of bad news. When asked if she had seen Mr. Wadsworth around or near the home, she said she had not.

"I spread old newspapers on the table in the dining room, you see. 'Tis the only one large enough to lay the silver out for polishing, and I always keep the door closed. I've my own recipe for silver polish, don't you know. Works a treat but smells something awful."

"You saw no one enter the house?" The coroner looked as if he'd aged a few years as Mrs. Pratt told her story.

"I never saw that man." She pointed towards Wadsworth. "There was," Mrs. Pratt cast her eyes downward, "a moment when I left my post to…ah…attend to a private matter, don't you see? As I returned from the water closet, I saw the master admit a lady into the house."

Mrs. Pratt paused dramatically, an expectant expression on her face as if she were waiting for a collective gasp to erupt from the crowd. She appeared disappointed when all that could be heard was the shuffle of a few feet and a cough from somewhere near the middle of the chamber.

"I didn't recognize her then, I didn't, but she's here in the courtroom today—and she's sitting right over there," Mrs. Pratt pointed, and every eye in the room followed the path from the tip of her finger to where Arabelle Grey sat next to Margot Greene.

Unsure which one of them the maid had been pointing towards, the two women whipped their heads to stare at each other accusingly, and then back at Mrs. Pratt, who had finally managed to get her dramatic moment.

"Her, in the grey dress," Mrs. Pratt shouted above the din, causing Margot Greene to fall back against her seat and begin fanning herself with her hand. Next to her, Arabelle looked like a fish out of water, her mouth opening and closing but no sound coming out.

The crowd's rumbling rose a notch in volume, but before complete pandemonium ensued, a gavel banged sharply against the sound block, forcing a disgruntled silence to fall across the room. Hope flared in Rosemary's chest but diminished again when she peered at Wadsworth and noted his jaw was still set as if carved in stone.

Esme Prescott had turned even paler than she'd been before, her fingers curled tightly around the edge of the pew in front of her. She appeared as though she might rise and strike at Arabelle, but one of her companions held her off.

"Arabelle was with me that afternoon. She did nothing wrong." Constable Percy Turner's voice sounded harsh as he stood and nearly shouted to be heard.

Across the aisle, Arabelle's face had contorted into an expression of horror, her cheeks flaming red. She moved then as if to speak but was shushed by the coroner, who once again recited the details of Nathaniel Prescott's demise.

"The verdict," the coroner paused dramatically, "is murder."

The word echoed across the chamber delivered news that was not by any means unexpected, but even so, another collective gasp rippled through the crowd upon its delivery.

A brief conference between the coroner, Max, and Commissioner Gibson ensued, and then Max approached the podium.

"As a result of the testimonies provided today, it has been decided that Carrington Wadsworth will remain in police custody pending further investigation. Miss Arabelle Grey will be called upon to provide us with her statement, as will Constable Percy Turner, and we will adjourn until further notice."

Rosemary and Vera waited until the crowd had begun to disperse before approaching a stunned Esme Prescott. Ivy Gibson had come to sit beside her while the commissioner engaged in a hushed conversation with Max and the coroner.

"Hello, Esme," Rosemary said, touching the woman lightly on the shoulder. She turned her face, and Rosemary was forced to steel herself against the pain written there. "I'm so very sorry for your loss."

Esme's eyes welled with tears, but she nodded and thanked Rosemary for the sentiment.

Rosemary then greeted Ivy, expressing her wish for their meeting to be under different circumstances, and made polite introductions. "This is my future sister-in-law, Vera Blackburn, and my brother, Frederick Woolridge. They've grown quite close to Wadsworth and wished to show their support. I realize it looks as though he may be guilty, but I assure you he isn't the type to resort to murder."

Esme directed one last glare in Arabelle Grey's direction and then turned to Rosemary with resignation. "I don't believe your butler murdered my husband," she said, sounding as though the admission sapped what was left of her energy. "I don't know him personally, but I trusted Nate, and he went to Mr. Wadsworth for advice of some sort. I can't see any reason why their conversation would have turned sour enough to warrant...well, to warrant Mr. Wadsworth wanting him dead." It was all she could get out, and she sank back into the pew.

Ivy Gibson patted Esme on the shoulder and turned to Rosemary.

"Certain parties would be perfectly comfortable seeing your butler swing at the end of a rope, as I'm sure you well know. We would far rather see justice served." She reached for Rosemary's hand, pressing a card into her palm, never breaking eye contact as if in silent warning.

Rosemary complied, surreptitiously depositing the card in her coat pocket while wondering if Ivy's choice of words had anything to do with her husband's statement in the paper that morning.

"We'll see you soon. Bring your friend along if you'd like," Ivy said, sauntering off to find Commissioner Gibson without a backward glance.

"What on earth was that about?" Vera asked once they were back inside the car.

"I've no clue," Rose replied, pulling the card out of her pocket. "213 Cedar Street, London. Wednesday, 2:15. I suppose we'll just have to wait and find out."

Chapter Nine

Rosemary found it no chore to drag Vera out of the house on Wednesday, given the lure of the clandestine meeting with Ivy Gibson. She had posited several theories during the hours when Frederick was off earning his living running Woolridge & Sons, none of which sounded viable to Rosemary.

"Somehow, I doubt we're walking into an ambush, being inducted into a secret society, or have been invited to join a knitting group," Rose had made such replies more times than she could count before finally deciding that a smile and a nod would do.

"You do know where we're going, darling?" Vera repeated the question a third time as Rosemary drove slowly.

"No. I thought we would drive aimlessly and trust the fates to guide us there." Rosemary's smile took all the fire out of the retort.

Truth be told, she was more familiar with the area than Vera knew. According to the map Rosemary had consulted before setting out, both Betsy's block of flats and the address from Ivy's card bordered the same park. It wouldn't do now to tell Vera the wedding dress of her dreams was within a stone's throw of their destination. Better to keep today's business focused on Ivy's mysterious invitation.

Both women found it a bit of an anticlimax as Rosemary pulled to a stop in front of a building that had fallen into significant disrepair. Boarded up windows and doors faced the street, and it looked like no place either of them would willingly visit.

"Perhaps we've been played for fools," Rose commented as she pulled her car to the curb across the street. "It is the right place, isn't it? 213 Cedar Street. Is there another Cedar Street in London?"

"We've already checked the map, Rosie, and the house numbers. This is definitely 213." Just for good measure, she pulled out the card from Ivy

Gibson and reread the instructions. "What are we missing?"

Rosemary contemplated turning around and driving back home, but while she hemmed and hawed about it, a shiny black car turned into the driveway of number 213 and disappeared around the back of the building. Rosemary followed, she and Vera exiting the car just as a woman in a long coat entered a door at the rear of the building.

"It looks significantly less sinister from back here than it did from out front," Vera said, some of her excitement returning. "Let's go."

Inside the door was a small hallway holding only a console-style table badly in need of a good dusting, and another door from behind which emitted the sounds of a gathering. Before Rose could get her bearings, Vera flung that door open and then stopped short as she took in the scene before her.

Rosemary peered over Vera's shoulder and immediately understood the reason for her friend's surprise. They found themselves standing in an old gymnasium and gawking at a group of women wearing loose-fitting trousers, their hair piled atop their heads.

Two of the ladies stood facing one another, crouched low in what appeared to be a battle stance, their hands covered with leather boxing gloves. Rose stared while they circled, seemingly prepared to strike, but didn't get a chance to see how it all ended because Ivy Gibson had noticed her and Vera from across the room and hurried over to greet them.

"Welcome, Rosemary." The woman had a mind like a steel trap, it seemed, as she remembered Vera's name and bid her welcome as well.

"Whatever is going on here?" Rose asked, her voice filled with wonder. In one corner, a willowy woman walked, surefooted, across a balance beam and then jumped off the end, landing squarely on the ground with her arms in the air. Across the way, another set engaged in a wrestling match, one woman pinned to the ground beneath the leg of another.

Ivy guided Rosemary and Vera to where Esme Prescott sat on one of the risers, her breath coming in short gasps. "You've been nominated as a new recruit," Ivy explained as if the statement clarified anything.

"Is this some sort of vigilante group?" Rosemary asked, still in awe.

With a laugh, Ivy shook her head. "No, of course not. We leave the crime-fighting to our husbands. What we do here is learn how to protect ourselves. If the war taught us anything, it's that there won't always be a man around to save the poor damsel in distress." Her eyes rolled skyward, and a smirk twisted her lips.

Like this, with her hair tied back, she looked twenty years younger and more than capable of handling herself in a physical confrontation. Rosemary remembered how she'd admired Ivy's toned arms the night of the fallen heroes banquet, now understanding why she was in such good condition.

"I suppose you could say we're an anti-damsel group," Esme added to Ivy's explanation as she stood and smiled warmly—if a bit thinly—at Rosemary and Vera.

"Our husbands assume we're engaging in some form of arts and crafts." Her smile quickly deflated further as the implication of her words sunk in. Esme no longer had a husband who either did or did not pay attention to her extracurricular activities. It was clear she'd experienced one of those moments Rose vividly recalled—a moment where the reality of her life had been briefly forgotten only to come crashing back down upon her a fraction of a second later.

"I'll let you explain, Ivy," Esme said, wiping her eyes and then resting a hand on the older woman's shoulder. "I feel a sudden urge to hit something." She headed off in the direction of a cluster of punching bags hanging in one corner, leaving Rosemary with a sense of regret that she hadn't had access to this type of release in her own time of grief.

"How long has this been going on?" Rosemary asked Ivy while Vera's attention was captured by a group of women performing some sort of stretching exercises she'd never seen before. Vera wandered off, waving a hand to indicate she'd explore on her own.

Ivy directed Rosemary to a pair of folding chairs, and they made themselves comfortable. "A few years, now. We began as a comfort group for grieving war wives and would spend hours every week lamenting our poor fortune while consuming alarming numbers of cakes and scones. Someone suggested we ought to start another group for those who could no longer fit into our clothes, and then the idea sort of snowballed into something more. But, it was Esme who shifted our focus into self-defense. Adamant that a woman living alone ought to know how to fight off an attacker, she even invited Margot Greene. To be honest, we've lived to regret that decision. Margot can be quite cloying. She's absent today, and you ought to be grateful for that small mercy.

"Anyhow, I do apologize for the clandestine nature of our invitation. You must have thought we'd lost our minds, but you see, some of the ladies' husbands wouldn't approve of our activities. It's best we keep our little group under wraps."

Ivy's eyes flicked to Vera, who had already removed her shoes and was now walking tentatively across the balance beam with a girlish smile on her face. Rosemary nodded in understanding.

"You can trust Vera. In fact, she'll be quite disappointed she wasn't the mastermind behind this idea."

"Good friends are hard to come by," Ivy replied, nodding in Esme's direction. "She seems to be coping. I suspect she'll crumble before long."

Rosemary couldn't help but agree. "Once the investigation is over, most likely. People will stop fussing over her, and she'll realize how alone she is."

"That's the thing about fussing. One abhors the attention until it's gone and only then realizes what a soothing balm it really was. There," Ivy stopped, noting Esme's approach, "she's spent some of her anger. Perhaps now she's ready to talk."

Esme did appear, as well as flushed, somewhat burgeoned by the physical activity. She sat down and dabbed at her neck with a towel.

"I'm sorry about that," she said to Rosemary, "but I needed a moment to clear my head. I trust Ivy has filled you in on our little group, and while we're happy to welcome you and your friend into the fold, that isn't the only reason I called you here."

Rosemary had a sinking feeling she already knew the second reason but waited for Esme to continue.

"Like I said at the inquest, I don't believe your butler is responsible for my husband's death. They were friends, just as Mr. Wadsworth indicated, and Nate trusted him implicitly. In fact, that's why he called your home so many times. He wanted Mr. Wadsworth's advice regarding a work matter that had been troubling him for quite some time. That's all he would say to me, which was Nate's way, but he met with Mr. Wadsworth the day of the banquet and came home acting more like himself than he had in months."

At this, Rosemary nearly choked. "What? Wadsworth didn't mention that he'd met with your husband—in fact, at the inquest, he made it a point to say he hadn't seen Sergeant Prescott in years."

"I know," Esme replied. "It seems odd, doesn't it? I can only imagine that the subject of their conversation was one my husband didn't want anyone else to know about. I fear he chose not to share his work-related trials with me. Nate thought he was protecting me from pain and worry, but he didn't realize not knowing made me worry even more. Sadly, there's nothing that can be done about it now."

Working with Andrew, even in small ways, helped Rosemary stave off a lot of the same worries Esme admitted to having. Once again, she found herself thankful to have been married to an honest man who included her in all aspects of his life.

"My husband was the most meticulous, perceptive man I've ever known. Still, his aspect changed in unsettling ways following his promotion to sergeant. I can see now that he smiled less often," Esme said sadly. "If he believed Mr. Wadsworth trustworthy, that's all I need to know. I assure you Nate wouldn't have wanted an innocent man hanged."

"Thank you," Rose replied. "I can't tell you how much I appreciate you not jumping to conclusions."

"It would be nice if our police officers could do the same, wouldn't it?" Esme asked. "That's why I wanted to speak to you. You know how to conduct a murder investigation, and I believe you will explore more angles than will Inspector Whittington. He made it quite clear to me that he believes Black's escape and Nate's death are connected, but I don't believe it. There was a revolver strapped to the underside of Nate's desk. The police found it when they searched the study. Had Black entered our home, my husband wouldn't have hesitated long enough to let him get a shot off—and he certainly wouldn't have entertained a conversation with the man. No, he must have known his killer, been comfortable enough to let her into the study."

Esme's use of the pronoun 'her' let Rosemary know precisely where her thoughts were focused.

"Unfortunately, my view on the subject remains unchanged. I don't expect Inspector Whittington to pursue other suspects with any sort of gusto, which is, in my opinion, a mistake. If Arabelle Grey was in my home that day, I want to know why."

"And you've no idea what sort of business she might have had with your husband?"

Rosemary spent a moment pondering the interaction she'd seen between Arabelle and Sergeant Prescott at the banquet. While she couldn't ascertain the true nature of their relationship from her limited observations, she rather felt that what she had witnessed went beyond the bounds of casual acquaintance.

"She's been after Nate for months now, showing up at the house and sending letters. He said their relationship was of a professional nature." Esme's tone spoke eloquently of her thoughts on the matter. "Trust is the bedrock of a good marriage, so I had no choice but to believe him. I did not, however, feel compelled to do the same for Arabelle Grey."

Hell hath no fury, Rosemary thought as she watched Esme's face for signs of prevarication. Seeing none, she drew her attention back to the conversation, which had continued on without her full attention.

"—had his concerns about some of the men he considered his comrades," Esme said. "He never came right out and said as much, but I could tell he worried over the fate of the department."

Rosemary felt a little lost, having missed the beginning of the segue but listened without interrupting to ask for clarification.

"From what Nate let slip, I gathered your Inspector Whittington was one of the few he considered above suspicion. Nonetheless, even a good man can labor under a mistaken assumption. If the Inspector is correct, and Black is responsible for Nate's death, so be it. But if he's wrong, I need to know someone is willing to look elsewhere for answers. Will you be that someone?"

Remaining quiet and keeping her face impassive, Rosemary considered Esme's revelations with a fair amount of skepticism. She hadn't questioned Max's concern over the source of corruption in the department, but she'd been under the impression it was his suspicion alone. That Sergeant Prescott held a similar theory proved him an observant cop and made his death an even bigger tragedy.

Without waiting for an answer, Esme said, "Let the inspector continue searching for Black— his apprehension is of the utmost importance, of course." Esme shivered at the thought of the mass murderer. "It took Nate ten years to catch him, and he lost a friend in Benton Greene. He never got over that, and he'd been on tenterhooks waiting to see Black executed."

Rosemary understood the meaning behind the statement. "And now he never will. I'm truly sorry for that," she replied.

Esme swallowed the lump in her throat. "Yes, I believe you are. We're kindred in that respect, Ivy as well. I should thank my lucky stars I have her to lean on. But enough of the doldrums. It is my turn to lead a calisthenics session. Please, get acquainted with the ladies," she waved a hand around the room, "and think about my request. I'd feel much better knowing I've you on my side. I'm sure I can count on you not to discuss my husband's suspicions with Inspector Whittington."

"Of course, your secret is safe with me," Rosemary replied, then watched as Esme picked her way to a set of mats across the gymnasium before turning back to Ivy, who had remained quiet during Esme's odd request.

"That was quite unexpected," Rosemary said, shaking her head.

"I can't think why. You've developed something of a reputation, you know." Ivy's face was harder to read than Esme's had been. "It should be a simple matter to speak to Miss Grey and determine if she had a hand in Sergeant Prescott's death."

Rosemary arched a brow. "I rather think Esme has an entirely different question she'd like answered, as Constable Turner has already provided Arabelle with an alibi. I can't say I'd have picked him as the type of man a woman like her would take up with."

Ivy responded with a conspiratorial look. "Arabelle is the type of woman willing to overlook a man's more unattractive attributes so long as he fills out his kit nicely."

A snort nearly escaped Rosemary's lips. "You might be right. I didn't hear her deny his statement at the inquest, so I can only assume they were together during the time in question."

Ivy sighed. "As Esme said, men will lie. Some for gain, some to cover their sins or those of others, and a good many will lie for the sake of a woman. A man like Percy might find more than one reason to speak an untruth."

Leaving that puzzling statement to hang in the wake of her passage, Ivy made the excuse that she was needed elsewhere. Sitting alone, Rosemary took a moment to wonder whether Ivy always spoke in riddles. The only clear point was Ivy's obvious dislike for Constable Turner.

With more questions rattling around in her head than she'd had at the beginning of the excursion, Rosemary set about the task of dragging Vera, forcefully, out the door.

"I promise, next time I'll participate. I'm looking forward to it, in fact," Rosemary assured her friend. "But for now, I have too much to think about. If Max's supposition that Black is responsible for Nathaniel Prescott's death is wrong, it means there isn't anyone looking for the real killer."

Vera stopped walking towards the car and placed her hands on her hips, tilted her head to one side. "I knew this would happen, Rose, and I don't think you should mount an investigation this time. It's not a good idea. What if it *is* Black and you get too close? You could be killed! You're exactly his type."

Rosemary rolled her eyes and sighed at her friend. "Didn't I just say I was going to look into who *besides Garrison Black* could have killed Sergeant Prescott? The first step, at Esme's request, will be to verify Arabelle Grey's alibi. How dangerous could it get?"

"Arabelle Grey is Esme's prime suspect in the caper?" Vera appeared surprised but recovered quickly. "With what motive? The old *if I can't have him, no one can* gambit? I suppose it could have happened like that, but I can't help thinking the scorned woman is such a cliche. Hasn't that been done to death?"

"Only in plays, dear one. Cliches surely turn out to be true more often than not, or they wouldn't be cliches," Rosemary reminded, to which Vera, for once, had no smart reply.

CHAPTER TEN

Rosemary didn't sleep well that night, either. The nightmares that had been plaguing her reached a crescendo, continuing to haunt her even after she'd descended to the dining room for breakfast and caught sight of the headlines in the morning paper.

"*Mass murderer still at large! London constabulary under fire.*" The article dubbed Black as "this century's Jack the Ripper" and hinted at gross incompetence within the police department.

Further down the page, beneath a brief description of the connection between Sergeant Nathaniel Prescott and Garrison Black, loomed a photograph of Wadsworth along with a grim prediction that soon, his guilt would be unequivocally proved.

The dark irony of mentioning both crimes while ignoring the possibility of a common culprit made Rosemary want to march into the press offices and kick up a fuss the likes of which they'd never seen before. Instead, she continued reading, her scowl becoming more pronounced all the while.

This time, the description of Black's calling card included a photograph, and the sight of it made Rosemary's stomach turn. It resembled a heart—albeit a shriveled one—and reminded her of another task she'd yet to complete: returning Betsy Brown's telegram. She hoped the carved hearts Betsy had described didn't resemble the one from Black's card and then pushed the thought from her mind with a shiver.

Her own heart taking up residence in the pit of her stomach, Rosemary worried over Wadsworth's fate as she sipped a cup of now tepid tea and pushed an uneaten square of toast around her plate. She regretted having been dissuaded from her intention of interrogating Commissioner Gibson almost as much as she regretted agreeing to Wadsworth's unreasonable demand for her to stay away from the jailhouse and vowed to right both wrongs at the first opportunity.

129

When the doorbell jingled from the other room, Rosemary hollered out to Helen that she would answer and then proceeded to do so. Her mood improved slightly when she found her next-door neighbor and good friend, Abigail Redberry, standing on the front stoop.

"Come in," she invited, leading Abigail towards the dining room. "Have a cup of tea."

Abigail hung back and tossed her head in the direction of the parlor door. "Why don't we talk in here. I've something to tell you, and it would be better to do so in private."

The statement, along with Abigail's serious tone, caused Rosemary's spirits to plummet once more. She felt as though, lately, her heart didn't beat but instead swung back and forth like a pendulum. "What is it now? I'm not sure I can stand another startling revelation."

"It's not quite as bad as all that," Abigail assured. "However, I feel I must inform you of a bit of gossip that's been circling, considering it involves your poor butler. Martin and I are still in shock, and we stand firmly behind you and behind Wadsworth. He's simply not the type to go in for cold-blooded murder. On that point, I' d be willing to testify."

While it did ease some of the rough edges to hear her friend offer such a show of support, Rosemary raised one eyebrow and waited for the inevitable 'but.'

"However," Abigail said, choosing a fancy 'but' but a 'but' nonetheless, "it seems not everyone in your household has such faith. My housekeeper is quite chummy with your cook. She mentioned that Helen has been rather loose-lipped about Wadsworth' s case and that, in fact, Helen is thoroughly convinced he' s been rightfully accused. Not only that," Abigail continued despite the stormy expression already pasted on Rosemary' s face, "but apparently Helen has been offered a small sum of money by one of the *Herald* reporters in exchange for confidential information about you, Wadsworth, and the investigation."

Rosemary could barely contain her shock, her eyes bugging further and further out of her head while Abigail spoke. "Thank you for telling me," she said rigidly. "I knew Helen had it in for Wadsworth, but I didn' t realize how deep her hatred ran. If you'll excuse me, Abigail, I feel I ought to go and rectify the situation immediately."

"Give me to the count of five to exit with all my limbs still attached." Under normal circumstances, Abigail's quip would have elicited a smile from Rosemary, but she was bubbling with too much anger.

She stalked out of the parlor, leaving Abigail to see herself out, and after allowing the door to slam loudly behind her, rounded upon Helen in the kitchen.

The spoon with which Helen had been stirring the stew fell to the floor with a clatter, spraying beefy sauce all over Anna who had, unfortunately, been carrying a load of freshly laundered linens to the servant's staircase on the other side of the kitchen.

Helen whirled around in surprise, her ruddy face pinched tight, mouth open as if preparing an onslaught that was quickly circumvented by one of Rosemary's own.

"I'm afraid our working relationship has come to an end, Helen. I've just been made aware of your indiscretions. To say I'm disappointed would be a gross understatement. I'm letting you go, effective immediately. Don't bother asking for a reference, either," Rose continued, holding her hand up and shushing the cook before she could speak. "I can't say I'd recommend someone willing to divulge house secrets, which you clearly have done or planned to do. Furthermore, if one iota of either fact or fiction regarding anyone in this household—including Wadsworth—sees the light of day, you can rest assured you won't be fit for hire anywhere in England. Of that, I'll make absolutely certain."

Anna's eyes went the size of saucers, and she glanced between the two possible exits looking for an easy escape. Realizing there was no way out, she kept her gaze trained on the floor as if hoping it would open up and swallow her whole.

"Just as well," Helen retorted, her voice full of vitriol. "I'd rather be out a job than stay on at one where the mistress is content to harbor a murderer! You'll rue the day you refused to see the truth, I tell you."

Rosemary thrust her nose in the air and held her hand aloft, her index finger pointing in the direction of the door. "Leave, now," she said icily, her expression dissuading Helen from saying another word. The former cook huffed, took her coat from the rack, and left with an even louder slam of the door than Rosemary had made upon her entrance.

"Well, Anna, it seems as though it's just you and me," Rosemary smiled wryly at the girl. "Don't worry, dear girl. I shan't make you cook for me," she added when she noted the look of horror on her maid's face.

Anna breathed a sigh of relief. "It's for the best unless you've a taste for cheese sandwiches. It's the only thing I can do proper. Everything else comes out terrible. Shall I call the service and see if they can send someone else over?"

"No, Anna, don't trouble yourself. I'll make the call. Actually, It's just occurred to me I've another to place as well. And I do apologize for the linens. Perhaps you can scrub the stains out rather than starting all over again."

Anna's mouth turned up into a small smile. "Don't bother yourself about it, Miss Rose. It was worth the trouble watching steam come out of Helen's ears. For that, I'd do a dozen bucket loads of laundry."

Rosemary couldn't hold back a grin of her own and treated Anna to a conspiratorial wink before closing herself in the parlor and picking up the phone. She was forced to wait quite a while, but finally, the office manager came on the line and rather brusquely asked, "What can I do for you?"

After Rosemary explained the conundrum, he replied just as testily as he'd answered the call, "We've only one other cook available right now. Her name's Gladys, but I doubt you'll want to take her on."

"Whyever not?" Rose wanted to know.

The manager paused for a moment and then explained, "You see, she's colored."

Not even bothering to suppress an eye roll or her irritation, Rosemary snapped, "I don't see how that makes any difference. Can she cook?"

"Quite well, quite well," he replied, sounding somewhat jollier now despite Rosemary's acerbic tone. "She cleans, as well, at no extra charge."

"Then send her over," she demanded, slamming down the receiver and cursing out loud at how ignorant people could be. If Gladys was proficient enough to handle cooking and cleaning simultaneously, she'd pay her to do both jobs, and rightly so. "We've got a prospect, Anna," she hollered on her way back to the dining room. "Unless you've some objection to working alongside a colored lady."

Appearing surprised at the question, Anna replied, "Of course not, Miss Rose. None, whatsoever."

The matter having been settled, Rosemary made her second call on one Miss Arabelle Grey. She waited and waited for the operator to connect her, and was disappointed to discover that Arabelle hadn't answered. Rosemary surmised that the girl was either out or had stopped taking calls—likely the latter, as she was sure the press had descended upon Arabelle after learning what had happened at Sergeant Prescott's inquest.

With no other course of action, Rosemary decided a conversation with Miss Grey would have to wait, whether she liked it or not.

Gladys arrived in record time, her smiling face a welcome sight after Helen's perpetually dour expression. Soft of voice, neat in appearance, and capable of whipping up a meal with an economy of motion, she settled into the household as if divine providence had directed her to be there.

Rosemary left her teaching Anna some basic cooking skills, thinking Gladys would do quite nicely. If she were wrong by some chance, at least perhaps now she wouldn't be relegated to eating cheese sandwiches for the foreseeable future.

Chapter Eleven

Letting Helen go lightened Rosemary's mood considerably, and so that afternoon when Vera tried to ruin it again by waxing on about the possibility of eloping with Frederick, Rosemary made a snap decision.

"Enough of this. I propose we drive over to Betsy's house so I can return her telegram. I suggest you throw yourself upon her mercy and beg for the chance to buy that gown, and continue on with the original wedding plans. Otherwise, I will be forced to explain to my mother why you and Frederick have decided to break her heart. I'm sure she will forgive you. Eventually."

Vera didn't seem keen on the idea but took one look at Rosemary's face and decided this might not be the best time to push her friend. In token protest, she felt compelled to ask, "Didn't you say Betsy lives in a rather bad part of town? We promised Wadsworth we wouldn't go off by ourselves…"

"When has that ever stopped us before? I didn't hear you arguing over going to the very same area yesterday. I'll bring Andrew's revolver if it makes you more comfortable, but you're not getting out of this that easily."

Her tone indicated it would be wise for Vera to comply, and so she did, but with a nagging feeling that the mission wasn't going to be as easily accomplished as Rosemary thought.

Meanwhile, Rosemary wondered why her usually spunky friend had chosen to act the petulant child over a single detail of the wedding. An important detail, surely, but not one that would typically push Vera into doing something so rash as to flout convention.

"Why the rush to elope now? You're not…you know," Rosemary pointed towards her belly. "Are you? Because if you are, perhaps you ought to book a spot at the registry office directly as that would be a far worse notion for our mothers to accept. Living in sin is one thing; having a baby out of wedlock is quite another."

"I'm not with child, Rosemary," Vera replied icily. "Is it so difficult to imagine that I might, after years of denial, simply want to start my life with Frederick as soon as possible? Without all the fuss and expense."

Vera seeking to avoid a fuss went against everything Rosemary knew about her friend, who generally liked nothing more than to be the center of attention. Furthermore, she couldn't remember a time when the notion of *expense* had perturbed Vera either.

"I suppose not," Rosemary said reluctantly as she studied Vera's face for any clue as to why her friend had suddenly decided to throw out the baby with the bathwater.

"Besides," Vera continued, pretending to ignore Rosemary's searching gaze, "given the results of your investigation, I can't see what there is to gain by speaking to Betsy today. Nothing has changed."

Vera might have had a point. The day before, a message had been left for Rosemary stating that Betsy's Frederick Poole did not appear on the list of soldiers who perished in the war. She'd been assured that all variations of the name Frederick had also come up blank, forcing Rose to admit she'd hit a dead end. Without something to barter with, appealing to Betsy felt like a fruitless endeavor, but one of Rosemary's greatest assets was that of persistence.

"I still have her telegram, and I'm positive she would like it back. It can't hurt to try once more to persuade her to part with the dress, can it?"

"I suppose not," Vera sighed but agreed, knowing resistance was, at this point, futile.

By the time they'd pulled up in front of Betsy Brown's flat, though, Rosemary was relieved to see that Vera's spirits had lifted. If there was one thing that could be said about her, it was that Vera possessed more self-confidence than anyone Rose had ever met before. She also rarely backed down from a challenge—it was one of the attributes they both shared, and which had solidified their friendship—and this would be no exception.

Rosemary knocked on the door and waited, hearing a soft yowl coming from inside. "That would be the little hellion, Martini," she said, straining to hear footsteps or some indication that

Betsy was home. A few more moments of waiting left Rosemary feeling deflated as it became clear that Betsy either wasn't in or had refused to answer the door.

"She's out," came a voice from above the front stoop. An elderly woman poked her head out of the window over Betsy's flat and demanded, "What's your business with Miss Brown?"

"It's of a personal nature," Rosemary explained, reluctant to give any more information to a complete stranger. "We're friends."

The woman chuckled. "Now I know you're lying. Betsy doesn't have any friends to speak of. If it's urgent, I suggest you check the park down that way." She pointed and added, "Follow the river, and you'll find her." With that, she slammed the window closed with a bang.

"Well, then," Vera chuckled ruefully, shivering deeper into her coat. "It's rather cold for a walk, but I suppose we don't have much choice other than to sit here and wait. Or, we could simply go home and forget the whole thing."

It was one of those autumn days where the chill seemed to seep into one's bones and conjured images of sitting around a roaring fire with a good book and a cup of hot tea in hand. Yet, Rosemary refused to give up, her resolve solidifying in response to Vera's willingness to do so.

"This will probably be our last chance before the cold is too much to bear," Rosemary commented, "so why don't we enjoy the view and the exercise. Perhaps we will find Betsy, and perhaps we'll leave here with dress in hand!"

"Or perhaps I will freeze to death before we lay eyes on her," Vera grumbled, but retrieved a pair of gloves from her handbag and pulled her hat down over her ears. "However, I refuse to be labeled a wet blanket, so let's go."

Indeed the excursion did turn pleasant, watching the water of the Thames lap against the shore, the surrounding trees having turned to shades of green and gold. Upon arrival in the park, Rosemary searched each of the benches once before realizing Betsy probably wouldn't be wearing the pink dressing gown out in public—or at least not on such a crisp afternoon.

"Isn't that the back of the gymnasium where Ivy and her cadre meet?" Vera pointed. Rosemary pulled the image of the map from the depths of her memory.

"I think it is." She did another scan but still didn't spot Betsy. "I also think Betsy probably went on down the path already. Look, here, this must be the bench she talked about. It has a perfect view of the river, and see this," Rosemary pointed to a heart-shaped knot in the center of the seat. "It's exactly like she described."

Running a finger over the mark, Rose noticed the knot's perimeter had been drawn over in what she quickly identified as charcoal pencil. Over and over, someone had made a concerted effort to ensure the heart would stand out against the grain.

In two places, one at either end of the park, a footpath wound against the river's edge. "Which way?" Vera asked, edging towards the path to the left.

"No," Rosemary said, pulling her in the opposite direction. "It's this way. I'm getting a tingly feeling about it."

The pair ambled down the lane, a border of bushes and saplings partially obscuring the view, though every so often, a break in the foliage would allow a glimpse of the rippling water. Rosemary tromped right past one such gap in the trees, her eyes searching the way ahead for Betsy's figure. It took a few moments for her to realize Vera's footsteps no longer echoed behind hers.

"Rosie, look," Vera's voice came from the trees. Rosemary followed it, discovering that the spot she'd so hastily tripped past led to a small path that emptied out onto a lovely scenic overlook. But it wasn't the surroundings that had Vera's attention. She stood next to a fledgling maple and pointed at a knot outlined in charcoal—another heart-shaped knot like the one on the bench.

"This must be why Betsy walks down here so often," Rosemary commented, reaching up to run a finger over the shape. "To keep her Frederick alive in some small way. It's quite sad, really."

"Life is sad," Vera said dismissively. "We've all experienced loss. We'll all experience more. It's downright depressing, but it's true. What we must endeavor to do, Rosie, is focus on the positives. Things could always be worse. We could spend our time wallowing in the past like this poor Betsy, missing out on all the fun life has to offer."

For the first time all day, Vera sounded like herself, and somehow her words made Rosemary feel just a little bit lighter. Even so, she chose not to revisit or belabor the subject of a possible elopement—no matter how silly she believed Vera's reasons for its consideration in the first place. Better to persuade Betsy to part with the dress than to experience the maternal fury that threatened to descend should Vera and Frederick choose to marry in such a fashion.

The path continued until it looped back out to the main street, at which point Rosemary guessed Betsy had followed the footway back to her flat.

"I'm afraid my sense of direction has failed me. I've no idea which way to go to get back to the car from here, and we're losing light quickly. Shall we turn around and retrace our steps?"

Vera agreed, and by the time the pair returned to Rosemary's car, they were both shivering and could no longer feel their toes. Betsy's windows remained dark, and the last thing either of them wanted to do was wait for her return.

"I suppose we'll try again another day. For now, I say we go home and warm our feet by the fire," Rosemary suggested, then started the engine without waiting for a response.

She and Vera shivered their way into the house, collapsing onto the plush rug in front of the parlor fireplace. Frederick, who had been enjoying a pre-dinner glass of something amber-colored, smirked at his sister while wiping Vera's hastily-deposited lipstick kiss off his cheek.

"Whatever have you two been doing?" he wanted to know.

Rosemary explained and pulled the telegram from her pocket, only for Frederick to reach over and snatch from her hand.

"It's quite strange to see my own name on one of these things," he mused, fingering the slip of paper.

Rosemary made a move to retrieve it, but he yanked it away and held it closer to his face.

"There's something off about this telegram, Rosie," he said, turning it over and examining something only he could see. "Perhaps it's simply the passage of time, but the ink has faded considerably, and the paper is thinner than it ought to be."

"Since when do you know so much about ink and paper, brother dear?" Rose wanted to know.

His eyes still trained on the telegram, Frederick waved a hand. "One of my first projects at Woolridge & Sons had to do with overhauling the company letterhead. At the time, I don't think Father trusted me with anything more important than that, and now I'm practically an expert. Perhaps all that useless knowledge about typefaces and paper weight has finally come in handy. You should ask Max to take a look at this."

He handed back the telegram, and Rosemary examined it with renewed interest. If it wasn't legitimate, what did that mean for Betsy Brown? Furthermore, what did it mean for Vera's chances of acquiring the coveted dress?

Chapter Twelve

Still feeling the chill in her bones from the walk along the river, Rosemary retreated to her dressing room to prepare for an evening out with Max. His car was still being serviced, much to his irritation, leaving Rose with the task of driving them both to their hastily put together dinner date. She vehemently missed Wadsworth, not for the services he provided but for his ability to raise her out of the doldrums with nothing more than a few kind words.

Thinking of him caused a fresh set of tears to spring to her eyes, and she wiped them away impatiently. Crying wouldn't help Wadsworth now, and it seemed now was when he needed her most. Rosemary put on a stiff upper lip and ran through her list of suspects one more time.

Garrison Black, of course, was still an option. Finding and capturing him would kill two birds with one stone; get a mass murderer off the streets, and ensure Wadsworth's release. That is, if the fugitive confessed to the crime. Max had said that Black was arrogant and wanted the police to know he was responsible for his murders. He had, after all, left a calling card with each of his victims, which bore out Max's assessment.

Yet, there was still a chance Black would decline to take credit for Nathaniel Prescott. After all, he hadn't left his card at the scene of the murder, which could mean one of two things: either he actually *wasn't* responsible, as Esme Prescott believed, or he'd been interrupted by Wadsworth's arrival and never had the chance.

Based on Wadsworth's accounting, Rosemary was inclined to believe the former, even though it muddied the waters considerably by forcing her to review other suspects—suspects such as Arabelle Grey. If the Prescotts' maid was correct, and Arabelle had visited Nathaniel that day, she could be the murderer. And if, as his widow suspected, she'd fancied the man, and he rebuffed her, the motive was the oldest story in the book: *if I can't have him, nobody can.* Anyone with a finger could shoot a gun, and one wouldn't be difficult to come by for a girl like Arabelle.

However, if what Percy Turner revealed at the inquest was true, Miss Grey's motive grew more nebulous. Unfortunately, there didn't seem to be any hope of learning Arabelle's story with any sort of swiftness. Rosemary had tried several more times, unsuccessfully, to contact her, determining the girl either spent most of her time away from home or had simply refused to answer the telephone.

The, of course, there was Constable Turner himself. Ivy thought him capable of lying for Arabelle and of being tied to the corruption within the police ranks—at least, that's what Rosemary had gleaned from their short conversation. Would it not follow then that he could have been complicit in Garrison Black's escape? If so, he might also commit murder to cover up his own crimes. Maybe Sergeant Prescott threatened to expose Percy's duplicity. Or—and this was a stretch—perhaps they'd both been in on the corruption and had some sort of falling out.

In Rosemary's opinion, anyone who would perpetrate such schemes was probably capable of murder. Furthermore, she'd developed the impression Percy Turner had both hated and envied Nathaniel Prescott. She knew most policemen didn't habitually carry revolvers, but they certainly had access to one when needed.

From there, suspects and their motives became increasingly murky. She doubted the attack had been random, perpetrated by someone off the street, but the possibility still made her stomach churn. It was highly unlikely the killer would be found in that case, leaving Wadsworth to take the blame.

Rosemary also doubted very much that Esme Prescott was responsible, or—and this one was a stretch of the imagination—Ivy Gibson. Both were capable, and both had the means, but only Esme possessed what one would call a valid motive.

Of the two, Esme was the more likely suspect. One never knew what went on inside another couple's marriage, and her motive might well be related to some private conflict between herself and her husband. She certainly had taken a violent dislike to Arabelle Grey, and she'd given the impression she might not have trusted her husband as much as she professed to. Perhaps it was because she liked Esme, but even so, Rosemary rejected the idea. Why would the murderer ask her to investigate the crime? It simply didn't make good sense.

Ivy had no possible motive whatsoever, even if her name kept popping to mind every time Rosemary thought of possible suspects. Going back over the memories of her most recent encounters with the woman, only her penchant for veiled comments stood out as overtly suspicious, so Ivy's name went to the bottom of the list.

Rosemary glanced at the clock, cut her pondering short, and contemplated the rest of her plans for the day. Picking Max up from work did have its advantages. She hoped she might get a chance to speak to the commissioner and had composed a speech filled with irate expletives she'd never actually say aloud, knowing it would most likely have the opposite effect of her intentions. She could just as easily have sat in the car and waited for Max's shift to end, but instead, she arrived fifteen minutes early and hurried up the stairs to the third floor where his office was located.

Expecting to find the place buzzing with activity centered around catching Garrison Black, she was surprised to note the echoing emptiness of the station. It made her job a little easier, and she breathed a sigh of relief that was cut short when she noticed Percy Turner still sitting at his desk. He didn't appear poised to pack it in for the day anytime soon.

With a sigh, Rosemary vowed to avoid the man at all costs—a vow that evaporated as he caught sight of her and sneered.

"He's not at his desk right now, but I'm sure you can find him if you look hard enough," Percy said and then spat, "I trust you know your way around this department." The double entendre wasn't lost on Rosemary, who was so shocked and appalled at his audacity she didn't have time to respond before he proved her earlier conjecture wrong, rose and stalked away.

Still shaking from the encounter, Rosemary strode towards the door to the commissioner's office but stopped short when she heard furtive voices coming from the other side. One she recognized as belonging to Max, the other as the commissioner himself. She surveyed the room and noted the back of the last constable exiting to the stairs.

Rosemary took a seat in one of the chairs next to the commissioner's office door and inspected her nails while keeping her ears perked.

"Dammit, Max, you know I can't bend on this. They'll have my head on a platter if I give so much as an inch." Commissioner Gibson sounded more than a little agitated, but it failed at softening Rosemary's resolve to give him a piece of her mind. "If we show our cards now, we'll both be done for. You could start over; you're young enough for all that, but I'm not. I'm poised to retire at the end of the year, for God's sake."

Max's footsteps beat a path that Rose could hear from her side of the door as he paced back and forth. "How many lives have to be ruined before you decide to take a stand?" he finally asked.

"A stand against what? We don't know enough yet. We're close, but not close enough."

"I'm not suggesting we blow the investigation wide open, Alfie," Max retorted, "but the papers would have latched on to whatever statement they were given. Considering we have a mass murderer on the loose—one with a known grudge against

Nate Prescott—it seems as though coincidence goes out the window. How much more clear cut can it get?"

The commissioner huffed, "Perhaps you're right, Max, and Garrison Black is our man. Yet it can't be a *coincidence* that Carrington Wadsworth was at the scene of Prescott's murder either. That line about how they hadn't spoken in years. Hogwash, if you ask me. Those two were thick as thieves during Wadsworth's tenure. It's a shame he resigned; he was a good cop. Had he stayed on, it might have been him we were celebrating at that farce of a banquet. I hate to say it—ill of the dead, and all that—but I always had a strange feeling about Prescott."

"What kind of a strange feeling?" Max asked. Rosemary could tell his mind was racing when his voice changed from frustration-laced geniality to guarded suspicion.

"Well, for one thing, he couldn't let go of the past. That mention of Benton Greene during his speech is just one example. Greene's death was a sad turn of events, to be sure, but it happened ages ago. Furthermore, danger is part of the job, and Greene wasn't the only officer to fall during

Prescott's career. I'd say he chased Black for too long, got too caught up in the whole thing. I suggested taking him off the case, and he wouldn't hear a word of it. Said it was his duty to catch Black; that he couldn't let the man go free after killing on of our own."

"We all deal with the loss of a comrade in our own way," Max replied. "Sometimes, it lights a fire."

The commissioner grunted. "And sometimes it puts the fire out. You ought to know that better than most given your current...uh, situation. Andy Lillywhite lost his taste for police work, much like Wadsworth did after Greene's death. Andy wasn't there that night, but Wadsworth was, and he watched Greene take that bullet right alongside Prescott—"

"What?" Max demanded, interrupting. "Wadsworth was involved with the Black case? I had no idea."

"Oh, sure, sure. They both were, but Wadsworth's reaction was the polar opposite of Prescott's. Bowed out, resigned, and never looked back. Didn't have the stomach, I suppose, and probably didn't have the guts to kill Prescott either.

157

Unfortunately, my opinion doesn't make as big a difference as you'd like to believe. I don't possess unilateral power, much as I sometimes wish I did." He lowered his voice and continued quietly. "We're walking a fine line already, investigating our own men. We're taking a risk here. One that might be more dangerous than we thought. Furthermore, we aren't exactly keeping a low profile."

Rosemary stifled a gasp, her head spinning with a plethora of new information. She hadn't known about Wadsworth's past as a police officer prior to his arrest, and now it turned out there was more to the story. Rosemary couldn't see how this new knowledge would help solve Prescott's murder unless Max was right, and death had come at the hands of Garrison Black.

Whether or not that was the case, Rosemary couldn't think clearly while still reeling from the personal implications of what she had just heard. Any mention of Andrew would have perked her ears, but the commissioner's veiled suggestion he didn't have the fortitude for police work galled.

Even more exasperating, the realization her husband hadn't been as honest with her as she'd thought was a notion that disturbed her on several levels, not the least of which was that with him gone, she'd no choice but to wonder what other secrets he'd kept. She thought back on the locked desk drawer in Andrew's office and decided then and there that she simply must figure out how to open it. Even if it didn't hold the clues that would help Wadsworth's case, it would be one less unanswered question for her to fret over.

She came back to reality to hear Max say, "You can't deny, Alfie, that there's more to this case than meets the eye. Fingers have been pointed, and it's our job to find the truth—not a convenient end, particularly when that end would mean the gallows for an innocent man."

"If you're hinting at turning this investigation on its ear due to the ramblings of a near-sighted maid, you aren't the inspector I thought you were," the commissioner retorted. "Arabelle Grey's alibi is airtight unless you're suggesting you think Turner is some sort of turncoat. If you do, I disagree. He has neither the guts nor the brains to spearhead a sabotage campaign."

Max let out a derisive grunt. "I find it easier to believe he's playing both sides of the coin than that he caught the fancy of such a woman as Miss Grey."

Commissioner Gibson loosed a low chuckle. "Fine point, and one I don't entirely disagree with. However, for all his faults, I've never had a complaint filed against the man nor any evidence to suggest he's not simply a good cop with a bad attitude. For now, we focus on apprehending Black. He's too arrogant and too proud of what he considers his accomplishments," the commissioner spat, "to resist taking credit for Prescott's murder if he's the one responsible. Get a confession, and then we'll drop the charges against Carrington Wadsworth. It's the only way. You'd better do it quickly. Time is running out."

Rosemary winced at those words but sensed the meeting between the two men was coming to a close and decided it best if she made herself scarce. Max needn't know she'd been eavesdropping; would only admonish her for it and likely hold back any further details out of irritation or some sense of protection.

When he emerged from the building, she was there waiting in her car and made no indication that she'd been inside. His face set in stern lines, he slid into the passenger seat and presented Rosemary with a peck on the cheek, but when she made to drive away, he stopped her.

"I'm sorry, Rosie, but I can't have dinner with you tonight. I have...there are...I'm sorry. I just can't."

Rosemary thought Vera would be proud of how she schooled her expression to hide any prior knowledge of Max's current woes.

"It's quite all right, Max. I understand completely." More than he could possibly know.

His warm hand closed over hers. As it always did, his touch sent tingles along her skin and set her heart beating faster. He looked at her as though there were something he wanted to say but restrained himself to a reluctant goodbye.

Chapter Thirteen

Rosemary didn't even enter the living quarters of the townhouse when she returned from the station. Instead, she crept into the entryway and descended the stairs to Andrew's office before Vera or Frederick—who were most likely having a jolly good time pilfering her drinks cart—could notice she'd arrived home much earlier than planned.

She yanked open the desk drawer and removed its contents, then set about examining the smooth underside of the drawer in search of some sort of mechanism or inconsistency in the wood that might allow it to open. Positive she was onto something, Rosemary contemplated using one of her palette knives to pry the back away from the drawer but then thought better of it. It stood to reason Andrew would have wanted quick access to whatever he'd hidden inside, which meant there had to be an easy way to pop it open.

Before she could continue her examination, the telephone rang. Rosemary's eyes flicked to the clock above the door, and her brow furrowed when she noticed the time. Who on earth would be calling during the dinner hour? That notion that the call might have something to do with Wadsworth occurred to her as she picked up the instrument, held the speaker to her ear, and said, "Hullo," into the receiver.

"Rosemary Lillywhite, how could you?" Evelyn Woolridge demanded at a volume that caused Rose to pull the speaker back a few inches and roll her eyes skyward. "Why on earth you would encourage this nonsensical idea is beyond me. Are you trying to kill me?"

"Whatever are you talking about, Mother?" Rose asked mildly, though she suspected she already knew what had sent her mother into a tizzy.

Evelyn gasped. "Why, this *elopement*," she said, the word sounding like a slur. "It's absolutely ludicrous! Lorraine and I are considering disowning the both of them—you as well, as I know you must have had something to do with this."

How she was to be blamed for every one of Frederick's poor choices, Rose didn't understand, but it didn't surprise her in the least. "You should have talked them out of it," her mother said, her voice full of accusation.

"Mother, really. I don't know why you think I have any better luck with Freddie than you and Father do. And furthermore, don't you think I'm trying?" She'd hoped perhaps her brother and Vera had abandoned the idea, but it seemed as though that wasn't going to happen unless she could convince Vera to reconsider.

"I don't know what to think, except that none of you want me involved in your life. You've all traipsed off to London, leaving me positively bereft! My own children. How could you?"

"For goodness sake, Mother," Rosemary said, uncharacteristically speaking her thoughts aloud. Under normal circumstances, she thought it best to censor everything she said to Evelyn, but on this day, Rosemary found she'd left her patience elsewhere. "What would you rather have happen?

The two of them living in sin or being married in a registry office? Married is married, is it not?"

Her mother went silent, and for a moment, Rosemary thought perhaps she'd lost connection, but it only took another second for her to realize she'd let slip a detail Frederick and Vera had yet to reveal.

"You cannot be serious," Evelyn said, her voice quavering and then turning knife sharp. "Tell me you're not serious, Rosemary."

"Times have changed, Mother. It's perfectly common in certain circles for people to test the waters before making a lifelong commitment. I'll agree the point is somewhat moot considering Frederick and Vera have known each other since they were in diapers, but I can assure you their choices are not designed to hurt your feelings."

Her mother let out a rare, undignified snort. "Perhaps not; however, they're doing a lovely job of it all the same." Evelyn seemed to forget she was speaking to someone over the phone as she muttered to herself. Rosemary caught the words scandal, heathens, and a diatribe about her children trying to put her in an early grave.

"Nothing is set in stone. I'm doing my level best to convince Freddie and Vera to reconsider their plans, though right now, I'm more concerned about poor Wadsworth," Rosemary explained calmly, forcing Evelyn back down to earth.

Having released the pressure of her heightened emotions, Mrs. Woolridge went quiet for a moment before replying, "Yes, well, I suppose you do have quite a lot on your plate. Finding a new butler is a tiresome task. Would you like me to put out some feelers and see if I can secure you a replacement?"

Rosemary had to take a deep breath to avoid verbally tearing her mother's head off but couldn't keep the hard edge from her voice when she replied tersely, "I'm not looking for a replacement butler. Wadsworth is innocent, and as soon as I find proof of that fact, he's coming back here where he belongs."

"Of course he's innocent," Evelyn trilled in a tone that Rose knew well. It was the one her mother used when she disagreed with her daughter's opinion but also wanted to avoid an argument. "However, it's always best to be prepared."

"I'll take that under advisement, Mother," Rosemary said from between clenched teeth, what little patience she still possessed now entirely waned. "Meanwhile, why don't you and Lorraine put a temporary halt on your plans for the wedding. Give Vera some room to breathe. She's overwhelmed, and that's likely why she's taken Freddie's suggestion of elopement so seriously. They'd planned for a small, understated country wedding, not the overwrought spectacle you and Mrs. Blackburn have cooked up between you."

It was harsher criticism than Rose typically gave her mother, and had she not been so distracted by the idea of breaking into Andrew's secret drawer, she might have held her tongue.

Sure enough, Evelyn's tone went so cold the phone speaker seemed to take on the chill. "That girl has never done anything that could be labeled as understated. I can't imagine why she'd want to start with her wedding, of all things. I suppose I ought to be grateful I was allowed to help your sister with her big day, as I'm being thrust from Frederick's much as I was thrust from yours."

And there it was, the real reason for her mother's ire. "I realize that you were disappointed when Andrew and I decided we didn't want a big to-do; however, since I'm a widow now, perhaps you could dispense with the berating. I will do everything in my power to prevent Vera and Fred from running off and getting married without you. If I can accomplish that, I don't want to hear another word about my own nuptials. Ever again. Now, my tea is getting cold. I'll speak to you later, Mother."

With that, she hung up the receiver, instantly feeling guilty for having lost her temper. For all of Evelyn's tut-tutting, she really did have her children's best interests at heart, and the last thing Rosemary wanted was to cause her one iota of pain.

She pushed the thought from her mind, vowing to make a heartfelt apology the next time her mother called and went back to what she'd been doing prior to the ringing of the telephone.

Rosemary ran her fingers slowly around the front face of the desk drawer once more, searching for anything that felt out of place. Finally, with an irritated grunt, she slammed it shut forcefully and then broke into a satisfied smile when the facing piece of trim fell open to reveal a hidden cubbyhole.

Inside the compartment rested a stack of four books bound in leather, each one slightly more battered than the last. To Rosemary's surprise, every page was filled with Andrew's handwriting, and for a moment she thought perhaps she'd found a set of case journals.

Leaning back in the chair, she chose the most tattered volume and began to read, immediately realizing that what she had found didn't have anything to do with his work.

"I met a girl tonight. No, not a girl—a lady. One with a beautiful smile to go along with her beautiful name: Rosemary. Mother always said Rosemary was for remembrance, and now I know she was right. Rosemary Woolridge's face has been permanently seared into my heart. I'll marry her one day if she'll have me."

Shock and awe had Rosemary flipping through the pages of what amounted to a chronicle of her and Andrew's romance. He hadn't been terribly consistent; for weeks, he might pour out his feelings across several pages, then abruptly stop writing for long stretches of time.

Questions raced through her mind: had he always kept a journal, or was this something he began doing at the start of their courtship? If it was the former, where were the rest of the volumes? Had he been embarrassed by the practice, and is that why he'd never revealed it to her? Or were there thoughts within these pages he hadn't wanted her to be privy to?

Regardless, Rosemary couldn't tear her eyes away from the words even though the pain of reading them would have taken her to her knees had she not been sitting in a chair. She closed the cover when she reached the description of the evening he'd asked her to marry him, feeling as though her heart might break into a million pieces.

Instead of moving on to the next, she opened the volume she guessed was the most recent installment and read through the last entry her husband had made.

"Dr. Chapman says I ought not to give it another thought; that I should go on with my life as if nothing has changed. He says it could be years—decades even—before I experience any symptoms. How does *one simply forget they've been handed what amounts to a death sentence?"*

The words caused another pain to shoot through her chest, but this time it wasn't grief but fear of what she would learn if she continued reading. Steeling herself, she plodded on.

"Today I tried to tell Rosemary about Dr. Chapman's diagnosis, but she was in such a state after learning the news that her sister, Stella, is going to have a baby that I couldn't bring myself to hurt her. We've been trying for two years with no luck, but Stella came back from her honeymoon with Leonard simply glowing. I watch my wife contend with the expectations and hardships of the female plight, and though she handles each obstacle with grace and humility, I know they take their toll. Perhaps I will take Wadsworth's advice and seek a second opinion before I trouble her with my own worries."

Rosemary slapped closed the cover and shoved the volumes back into the cubbyhole. Not only had her husband, the soul she'd trusted most in this world, lied to her, but he'd also confided in someone else.

She supposed Wadsworth was the best sounding board Andrew could have had, but certainly, it would have made more sense to inform his wife that he was in ill health? How long had he known, and had it anything to do with his resignation from the police department? It was the second time she'd asked a similar question in a matter of hours, and she was beginning to wonder if she'd really known her husband at all.

In fact, she was beginning to wonder if anyone ever *really* knew anyone at all, and the thought was extremely unsettling. When it occurred to her to wonder if Max had known, acid bile rose up to burn in her throat. Could she continue seeing him if he had?

As she ascended the stairs, she kept her eyes from scanning the portraits of her and Andrew. Right now, she didn't want to see his face—didn't want to look into those eyes that she now knew held secrets. Secrets she might never have the answers to.

CHAPTER FOURTEEN

A hand-delivered note from Ivy Gibson arrived along with the newspapers and Rosemary's post the next morning. Splashed across the headlines was an entirely new story that had bumped Wadsworth's arrest down below the fold.

Rosemary held back a shocked cry as she recognized the face in the photograph beneath the headline "*Woman accosted in London flat narrowly escapes gun-wielding intruder—identifies her attacker as escaped mass murderer Garrison Black!*" Arabelle Grey's face smiled at her from the page, and the implications of this new development pushed all thoughts of Andrew's secrets to the back of her mind.

"Well, knock me over with a feather," she said to nobody in particular, the house having become unusually quiet without Helen's constant chattering. The reprieve, she found, suited her nicely, and the sentiment was echoed when Gladys delivered her breakfast with a soft, "Here you are, madam, can I fetch you anything else?"

Gladys stopped, peered at the paper, and Rosemary's stomach turned over in anticipation. Instead of uttering some sort of derogatory comment as Helen would have done, she made a cluck-cluck sound and said, "Poor thing," before returning to the kitchen. Rosemary let out the breath she'd been holding in and decided that if Gladys was amenable, she could take the position of cook permanently.

When Vera finally made it to the breakfast table, Rosemary handed her Ivy's note with a raised eyebrow. Vera, not yet fully awake, squinted, read the message, and nodded. "It's a different place from the first," she said through a yawn.

"Did the Chelmsford address tip you off?" Rosemary quipped, receiving a grumpy glare in return.

"Do you suppose they meet in a different place each time?"

"I wouldn't think so," Rosemary replied, "and that gymnasium certainly didn't pop up overnight. I wonder who owns that property, come to think of it. Perhaps we'll find out today. Are you in?"

Vera nodded, this time through a piece of buttered toast she'd jammed into her mouth. When she had finished chewing, she said, "Wouldn't miss it. Those ladies are simply wonderful, though my thighs felt the strain after all that stretching."

She glanced at the paper, her eyes finally fully open, and made a comment similar to the one Gladys had—minus the clucking sound—before setting it back down and returning to her food.

"You don't recognize her, do you?" Rosemary asked, surprised. Vera usually remembered a face—especially one pretty enough to rival her own. "She's the one from the inquest. The one Inspector Prescott's maid accused of visiting the house the day he died. Her photo was in the paper the next day. Honestly, Vera."

After treating her friend to another scowl, Vera scrutinized the face staring back at her while rereading the story from a different perspective. "It says she was able to wake her upstairs neighbors with a bloodcurdling scream. The intruder was scared off by the neighbor descending the stairs and had fled by the time the police arrived. She was quite lucky."

"Quite lucky, yes," Rosemary said slowly. "Or quite unlucky, depending upon how you look at it."

"Whatever do you mean, Rosie?" Vera asked, trying to put the pieces together but coming up blank. "Has anyone ever accused you of talking too much first thing in the morning?"

"Honestly, Vera, a wet dishrag has more life in it than you do in the morning. Think for a moment."

"I'm trying," Vera huffed out a breath. "I still don't understand how that could be possible."

Rosemary grimaced, "She fits the description of Black's former victims quite perfectly, and furthermore was friendly—in one way or another—with Sergeant Prescott. I think it would be a stretch to imagine the two crimes aren't connected in some way. You see, I had made up my mind that Esme was correct in her conviction that someone other than Garrison Black was responsible for her husband's death. But, the conversation I overheard between Max and Commissioner Gibson got me wondering. There's more to this story, and the attack on Arabelle Grey makes me think perhaps Wadsworth's involvement wasn't entirely accidental."

"You think it was a frame job?" Vera asked, less bleary-eyed now.

"I think it's a possibility. If I knew for sure, I'd have Wadsworth out of jail by now. It just seems to me that the connection can't be a coincidence." Now, she sounded exactly like Commissioner Gibson, and it rankled. "Perhaps Max was right, and Black really is the murderer. Regardless, I've every intention of finding out. I think the meeting today is a good place to start. At the very least, I can speak with Esme again. With any luck, we'll come home with another clue."

"Good plan." Vera yawned again. "Remind me not to take on more stretching today. I'm rehearsing later, and I can't be too sore to tread the boards now, can I?"

As it turned out, stretching wasn't on the agenda for the day's excursion, although what exactly Ivy and the ladies had planned wasn't clear upon arrival at the sprawling country manor house an hour outside the city. A cacophony emitting from somewhere towards the back of the property disrupted Rosemary's admiration of the landscape mere moments after she alighted from the car.

A smartly dressed but harried-looking maid greeted the pair at the door and directed Rosemary and Vera to make their way around the side of the house. "Everyone is out back," she said sharply while smoothing her hair with a shaky hand. "Simply follow the racket. You can't miss them."

The maid was correct; there was no way to miss a group of trouser-clad women, all aiming various firearms towards the sky. Every few minutes, a new set of clay targets flew through the air, prompting another round of firing.

"Rosemary, Vera, over here!" Ivy Gibson yelled from across the lawn. "We're honing our firearm handling skills today"—she lowered her voice and glanced surreptitiously in Esme Prescott's direction—"in light of what happened to Arabelle Grey. Word is, she had a pistol but didn't know how to load it."

Where word had come from, Rosemary couldn't imagine, but Ivy's connections seemed nearly infinite, so Rosemary didn't spend much time pondering the source. Instead, she murmured,

"A close call, certainly," her eyes locked on Esme, "and quite interesting timing, wouldn't you say?"

Ivy's lips pressed into a thin line. "Quite. There's no denying that. Perhaps later we'll have a chance to discuss the threads connecting Nate's death to Arabelle's attack, but for now, why don't you two follow me. We've got rifles and pistols of various calibers and weights, and plenty of ammunition thanks to our generous but absent host and my good friend, Lady Weatherford-Fisk. We've the whole place to ourselves and have been instructed to do as we please. Now, have either of you ever fired a gun?"

Both Rosemary and Vera nodded, and Rosemary explained proudly, "My father taught us to shoot when we were young. He said he wanted us to be prepared for anything. Andrew kept the tradition alive, and we would practice when we visited my family's country house."

"Excellent. Some of these ladies have never had an opportunity to hold a gun, much less learn how to use one properly. Perhaps if Arabelle had been adequately trained, Garrison Black would be locked in a cell right now instead of prowling for his next victim—presuming, of course, it was he who attacked her at all."

"You don't think it was Black?" Rosemary asked with a raised eyebrow. One could never tell what Ivy might be thinking.

Ivy shrugged. "I don't know what to think, honestly. Arabelle, as far as I can tell, isn't to be trusted. She insists her relationship with Nate was completely innocent, yet Esme claims she'd been pestering him for months. I've known Esme long enough to know exaggeration isn't one of her faults. Therefore, I'm inclined to take everything Arabelle says with a handful of salt—including her alibi for the day Nate was murdered."

Rosemary allowed Ivy to return to her explanation of the day's activities, all the while thinking it mighty interesting that Esme still clung to the idea of Arabelle as the murderer despite the evidence to the contrary. Even disregarding the alibi altogether, which Rosemary tended to agree could have been coerced, had Arabelle decided to kill Nathaniel Prescott, it seemed unlikely she would have chosen a weapon she lacked the knowledge to use. The irony of the situation didn't escape Rosemary, and in fact, made her think she ought to take a closer look at Esme Prescott after all.

She peered at the woman from across the lawn. Esme was quite fetching in a thick waistcoat over long sleeves, the cold having little effect other than to turn her cheeks rosy and pink and force her fingers to rub together every so often. Rosemary even noted that she smiled genuinely while helping one of the other women aim her rifle and take a shot into the sky. When the bullet failed to make contact, and the kickback nearly knocked her over, she handed the gun back to Esme.

"Please try again," Rosemary heard Esme urge as she followed Vera towards the gathering. "It's natural to be scared, but we can't let fear control us. We must face it instead. Otherwise, it will take over our lives. And, I promise you, it will make you feel better to destroy something—even if it is just a clay target."

When shards of clay splintered and rained down to the ground, Esme patted the now jovial woman on the back and moved on down the queue in the direction of someone whose face Rosemary didn't have to see to recognize. Margot Greene, dressed in a deep forest shade that caused her to blend into the landscape—not the smartest choice for the day's activity—stood back and watched as the others handled their weapons with various degrees of comfort.

"Are you in need of instruction, Mrs. Greene?" Rosemary heard Esme ask over Vera's chattering. She pushed her friend in Ivy's direction and continued on her original trajectory.

"Not hardly," Margot Greene replied. "I *was* the mother of a cop, after all. Benton taught me to shoot when the grey squirrels began to overrun the garden."

Esme started and stuttered, "but the squirrels are adorable, with their little paws and fluffy tails."

"Ha, adorable," Mrs. Greene scoffed. "They are terrible pests and will stuff nuts into every nook and cranny they can find. One even burrowed its way into my attic and ate through one of the roof supports. The only way to stop it is to kill them, one way or another. Rat poison works, but the problem there is they eat it and then crawl into the walls or ceiling and die. Trust me, the smell of decomposing squirrel is not pleasant. Better to kill them quickly, and more humane if you're a good enough shot."

As an example, she smartly blasted another clay target before placing her rifle back on the rack. "Don't you worry about me, dear. I'll help some of the other ladies while you take a break. You're looking a little peaked."

In fact, Esme did appear a bit paler than she had before, and when she turned around and came face-to-face with Rosemary, she let out a nervous, high-pitched laugh. "Did you happen to overhear any of that?"

"Yes," Rose replied. "It was enough to put you off your luncheon, wasn't it?"

"Certainly so," Esme said with a little shake of her head. "Though somehow not surprising coming from Mrs. Greene. She's always had a hard edge, but she means well enough."

Relieved at the thought if Esme couldn't stomach the idea of shooting a squirrel, she probably hadn't murdered her husband, Rosemary felt the butterflies in her stomach slow the beating of their wings. "How are you doing, really?" she asked as they walked.

"Honestly, I don't know. It helps to have a distraction, but of course, I haven't stopped thinking about Nate's death for one second. Tell me you've found something useful," she said, a plea in her voice.

How she would have discovered anything useful with absolutely nothing besides conjecture upon which to base her inquires was a mystery in itself, but she replied gently, "I don't believe Arabelle is responsible—and I don't think you really do, either, given what's happened to her recently. Had she owned or known how to use a gun, Garrison Black would be dead right now."

Dead, and unable to confess to your husband's murder, Rosemary added internally. That wouldn't have done at all, but she wouldn't say as much aloud.

Esme's face contorted at the sound of Arabelle's name, and she looked as though she could spit. "Unless she's lying again. Perhaps there was no intruder at all, and this whole story is a ploy to make herself appear innocent."

"It's possible, of course," Rosemary hedged, astounded at the lengths Esme was prepared to go to pin the murder on her favored suspect. "I certainly haven't discounted the prospect. However, as with any murder case, it's important to remain objective and consider all angles. Which is exactly what I wanted to discuss with you. I hate to ask, but did your husband have any other enemies besides Black? I'm sure his escape was difficult for Sergeant Prescott to accept."

Again, Esme's expression turned into one of deep pain. "Nate rarely made enemies; he was far better at making friends. However, with regard to Black, Nate carried more guilt than anyone would have known."

"Are you referring to the death of Benton Greene?" Rosemary asked though she suspected she already knew the answer to that question.

Esme nodded and swallowed hard. "Greene's death was a touchy subject for him. It happened long before we married, and he didn't care to discuss it, but when Black reappeared a few months ago, Nate...changed, somehow. All he told me was that six years ago, the attempt to capture Garrison Black shouldn't have gone the way it did. Benton wasn't merely a comrade. He was Nate's friend. I can't see how it matters now."

"It likely doesn't," Rosemary assured, "but you know what they say about stones unturned."

"I wish now I had thought to ask. One never does ask the important questions, does one?"

The sentiment struck home so squarely that Rosemary had to bite the inside of her lip to keep the tears that had sprung to her eyes from spilling down her face.

"I suppose not. For that, we'd have to know what the important questions are in the first place," Rosemary commiserated. "Now, all that's left is to sort things out for ourselves. Having a group of like-minded ladies to lean on is a blessing. I had Vera, and my brother, Frederick, of course," she peered across the lawn and watched as Vera aimed for a target, "but little to pass the time and even less to smooth the sharp edges that come along with sudden loss."

It wasn't until later that she thought back on the conversation and recalled the look on Esme's face when she had mentioned *important questions*. It had been one of grief and pain, certainly, but there had been something else. Regret, perhaps, for the questions she hadn't asked. Or, and Rosemary shivered as the thought crossed her mind—it could have been guilt.

Chapter Fifteen

Rosemary dropped Vera off at the theater for play rehearsal and then returned home to find Anna tidying her bedroom, a fire already roaring in the grate. "Bless your heart," she thanked the girl and moved closer to the flames, reveling in the warmth after a day outdoors in such crisp weather. A brief explanation of her movements sparked interest and then skepticism from the young maid.

"Guns scare me, though not as much as do knives," Anna said with a shiver, no doubt remembering the brush she'd had with death on holiday in Cyprus only a few short months before. "No, I dare say I would be too scared to try shooting."

"That's exactly why you should. Perhaps I'll take you some time."

Anna declined to respond, instead refocusing her attention on assisting her mistress with preparations for the evening. "How about this one?" she asked.

"That might do," Rosemary replied, taking the hanger from Anna and holding a black fringed cocktail dress up for inspection. "I'll have to liven it up a bit," she mused. "Perhaps a few strands of pearls or that outrageously expensive necklace Vera bought me. Yes, I think that will be just the ticket."

"Inspector Whittington will be thunderstruck," Anna predicted.

Rosemary murmured her agreement noncommittally. Better to let young Anna believe her mind occupied by romance; the girl would learn soon enough just how duplicitous a woman must sometimes learn to be. That evening, she intended to pry the truth out of Max, a prettily made-up face and a scandalously short skirt her wrench of choice.

Having finally retrieved his car from the repair shop, Max arrived sans sweaty armpits and in a far better mood than he had the evening of the fallen heroes banquet. Once again, the hollow echo of

Wadsworth's absence drained his spirits slightly, eliciting an uneasy feeling that he was running out of time to clear the man's name.

"Well, hello gorgeous," he said with a whistle, Rosemary's appearance obliterating all thoughts of aging butlers and murder investigations from his mind.

He couldn't stop glancing appreciatively in her direction during the ride across town, eliciting a pang of guilt she made an effort to push aside. If Max had kept Andrew's secret from her, were there others? What else might he be withholding? Some wives might have been content to accept the little day-to-day things her husband wouldn't tell her, but Rosemary had not been one of those wives, and she refused to be that type of paramour either.

Max parked, opened Rosemary's door, and held out his arm, pointing to a warmly-lit restaurant half a block down the street. The scents of oregano, garlic, and freshly baked bread wafted out to meet their noses as diners—appearing duly sated— exited the glass-fronted door. Max's stomach rumbled with anticipation.

"Something smells positively heavenly," Rosemary commented, taking a deep breath and smiling at Max more easily than he'd seen her do for some days. Tension still gathered her brows together, and he could tell she'd something on her mind, but the momentary softness gave him hope she hadn't tired of him just yet.

"Indeed," Max replied, then took her hand in his and didn't let go until they arrived at a cozy table for two near the back of the restaurant. He requested a G&T while Rosemary opted for a dry martini, and then they were left to peruse the menu.

Positioned as he was—a cop's habit, surely—with his back to the wall, Max enjoyed a full view of the restaurant. Enjoyed, that is until he spotted a familiar figure hunched over the bar. He stiffened and hoped the man would finish his drink and leave quickly.

Rosemary, oblivious to anything except Max's demeanor, felt a chill when he abruptly let go of her hand. She wanted to ask what had made him go rigid but found she wasn't sure she wanted to know the answer just yet. Instead, she gulped down half of her martini, felt it hit her stomach with a slosh, and then go straight to her head.

Rather than slow it down, as her conscience (and the voice of her mother) would usually dictate, she took another generous sip.

"Rose—" Max said at the same time she opened her mouth to begin what she feared would turn into an uncomfortable conversation. "Max—." They both stopped at once and then broke into twin smiles that helped thaw the ice.

"Go on," she said with a wave of her hand.

"No," he replied with a resolute shake of his head. "Ladies first."

Rosemary realized, somewhat foggily through the gin-induced haze, that she hadn't the first clue what she'd initially intended to say.

"I know why you're upset," Max said, jumping to the most logical conclusion. "Wadsworth ought to have been released by now, and I'm terribly sorry it's taking so long to set things right."

Before she could respond, the waiter returned with a second round of drinks, adding an apology to the mix when he explained that their meals wouldn't be ready for several more minutes.

"You presume too much, Max," Rosemary announced once the waiter had scurried off again. "I'm devastated by Wadsworth's situation, yes, but that isn't the only reason for my behavior."

While sipping her second martini, she explained about Andrew's diaries and the questions he could never answer for her now.

Rosemary needn't have been stone-cold sober to recognize the genuine shock on Max's face when he realized his best mate had been aware of his supposedly undiagnosed heart condition for quite some time before his death.

"I can understand why you feel betrayed," Max said, reaching across the table to take her hands in his again. "You've more a right to that than I, and yet it makes me angry."

For a moment, there was complete silence before Rosemary surprised him by smiling. "You didn't already know, then? I can't tell you how relieved I am to hear it."

All of the fear and worry she'd been carrying around suddenly fell away, leaving Rosemary feeling the full effects of the second martini, which by then had been depleted by well more than half.

"Excuse me," she said to Max, "while I powder my nose."

He nodded, appearing concerned but certainly unwilling to press the issue, while she made her way to the loo with as much grace as she could muster. A few long minutes later, she emerged feeling somewhat better but still rather tipsy and even more ravenous than before.

Thoughts of tender, sauce-coated pasta strands danced through her mind as she hurried in the direction of the table. Her stomach turned to acid, and Max's hopes were dashed when she recognized the head of disheveled hair and hooked nose of Percy Turner leaning over the restaurant bar.

Spurred on by her current state, along with the lingering irritation over Percy's remarks during their last encounter, Rosemary stalked in his direction. By the time the man realized he ought to have paid more attention to his surroundings, it was too late.

She leaned in close, still cognizant enough to wish to avoid making an entirely public scene and demanded through clenched teeth, "Who do you think you are to comment on my relationship with Max Whittington? Furthermore, who are you to make judgments regarding the length of time I'm required to mourn my dead husband?"

Though taken aback, Percy wasn't quite as dimwitted as he appeared, and he fired back, "Touched a nerve, did I?"

Rosemary herself was surprised when Max, evidently having decided she'd been gone from the table long enough to warrant a search party, popped up out of nowhere and squared off to face Percy with fire in his eyes.

"You touched one of *my* nerves, Turner, and as it happens, I've yet to exercise any of the benefits that go along with being named chief inspector. I'm quite content to rectify that oversight."

Percy sneered, "Standing up for your little lady, I see. Doesn't surprise me; she looks the type to need rescuing."

"It's obvious to me that you don't know the first thing about Rosemary, then. In point of fact, she's usually the one doing the rescuing," Max said, speaking slowly and calmly as though Percy were a misbehaving child.

Which, to Rosemary's mind, he was indeed, and proved it further when he snapped back, "If that's the truth, then why is her butler still rotting behind bars?"

The argument was beginning to draw nearby diners' eyes, along with a few glares from the wait staff. The fire of her anger had mostly burned the gin from her veins, leaving Rosemary feeling quite foolish, but Percy's next statement fanned the flames.

"At this rate, he'll have been hanged long before she gets around to the rescuing part, but I suppose that will be appropriate for an old coward like Carrington Wadsworth."

Max's eyes flashed, and his fists clenched at his sides, but it was Rosemary who spat, "What exactly do you mean by *coward*?" Of all the words Percy might use to describe Wadsworth, coward wasn't one she expected.

Percy's hubris deflated as his face reddened, further piquing Rosemary's curiosity. He mumbled something unintelligible and made as if to rise from his stool, only to be forced back onto it by Max's hand on his shoulder.

"Apologies, *Chief Inspector*," Percy spat. "But I have nothing more to add."

"Answer the lady's question. Now." Max reiterated, his inspector's senses having kicked into overdrive. Percy was hiding something; Rosemary knew it, and so did he, and neither of them was willing to let the subject drop until they'd discovered precisely what it was.

"You won't get anywhere with threats," Percy replied. "I won't break an oath made in good faith. Your beloved Wadsworth certainly wouldn't appreciate it, and though it would give me great pleasure to do so, I simply won't. Arrest me if you think you have reason," he challenged.

When Max's jaw tightened, and a defeated expression covered his face, Percy sneered. "That's what I thought." He removed his billfold, placed a stack of notes on the bar, and left with one last jab. "You want to know the truth, ask old Wadsworth yourself."

By the time she and Max returned to their table, their food had been delivered and gone cold. Rosemary's appetite had flown, so Max paid the bill, neither of them speaking until they were inside his car and halfway back across town.

"This evening didn't go exactly as planned, did it?" Max asked with no hint of amusement.

Rosemary shook her head and said in a voice so low it was almost a whisper, "No, not exactly." She was silent for a moment and then, as if having regained her strength, pleaded, "Max, you have to allow me to speak with Wadsworth, whether he likes it or not. It's the only way to get to the truth, and something tells me we need to discover it quickly, or Wadsworth will be branded a murderer and his days numbered."

Max had to admit she was right, even though he'd convinced himself that saving Wadsworth would be as easy as capturing Garrison Black— which, ironically, turned out to be an accurate assessment, as he was failing just as spectacularly at both.

"All right, Rose. You win. I'll let you in, but you're taking the blame with Wadsworth, not me."

Chapter Sixteen

Rosemary stayed awake long after Vera, tired of discussing murder, had gone up to bed. She paced across her bedroom floor until she nearly wore a path into the carpet, running through what little evidence she had to go on and hoping for an epiphany to strike.

She finally fell into a fitful sleep sometime during the wee hours of the morning, but it hadn't amounted to much. Still, she arrived at the jailhouse fresh-faced and impeccably dressed.

Max greeted Rosemary outside the entrance and made one last appeal. "You don't have to do this. I can speak to Wadsworth myself. Then we both get what we need, only he doesn't flog me after he's been released."

"Max, you know me better than that. Lead the way," she said resolutely, the fire in her eyes telling him all he needed to know.

He did as he was told, wondering briefly if being ordered around by Rosemary was to be his fate and deciding if it was, he'd accept it with a smile on his face. Whether he would live to regret that decision once Wadsworth got to him was the question.

"Chief Inspector Whittington to see Carrington Wadsworth," he told the clerk at the desk, who made a big show of checking his list despite the 'Chief Inspector' title in front of Max's name negating the necessity to do so.

"Got to be careful these days. Can't let just anyone in, you know," the clerk said as though he were the gatekeeper to the Emerald City.

Max schooled his annoyed expression as he led Rosemary down a long hallway to a large room that smelled of rancid sweat and held an assortment of the most wretched-looking men she'd ever seen. Why Wadsworth hadn't wanted her to visit was quite obvious now, and she had to remind herself that she had made the right decision whether he agreed with it or not.

Rosemary stayed behind Max, slightly hidden until they reached the rough wooden table Wadsworth sat behind, perched on an equally crude three-legged stool. Aside from the day at the courthouse, she couldn't remember a time when she'd seen him sit; he'd always towered grandly over her, waiting to do her bidding.

What did she really know about this man? Rosemary wondered. The thought was a sobering one but did nothing to diminish either the affection she felt towards him or the concern she had over his current predicament. His glare when she stepped out from behind Max accomplished more on that front, and any question she might have had as to whether Wadsworth could appear forbidding was decidedly answered.

"Please don't be cross with me," Rosemary said softly. "I had to come. There are questions to which only you know the answers."

Wadsworth remained seated and silent, appearing to consider her statement. Finally deciding to acquiesce, he motioned for her to take a seat across from him, which she did, visibly relieved.

"Are you all right? I mean, of course not," she stuttered, "but are they treating you well?"

"I'm quite well," Wadsworth replied, "save for the humiliation of you blatantly disobeying my wishes." It was a day of firsts, and the only time he'd ever spoken to her without the respect of a servant. "However, I suppose I should have expected as much."

Rosemary felt the temperature rise as Wadsworth thawed infinitesimally despite his words.

"You have nothing to be ashamed of," she assured him.

He declined to reply, instead pressing his lips into a thin line and motioning for her to say whatever it was she so desperately needed to say.

"I'm aware you'd prefer if I stayed out of this, but I also know you'll understand that I am simply incapable of doing so. I know you lied at the inquest when you said you hadn't seen Sergeant Prescott in years. His wife seems to believe the two of you had lunch on the day of the banquet. It was you he was waving at that night, not Max, was it not?"

After a deep sigh, Wadsworth nodded. "Yes. We had lunch. We talked, and I did what I could to ease his mind. I'm glad I did so now, in case I brought him some peace before he died. But at the time, I was bitter. You see, I left police work for good reason, and I didn't appreciate the past being dredged up after all this time. Nor do I prefer it being dredged up now."

Rosemary felt a pang of guilt but refused to allow it to dissuade her from learning what she needed to know. "What did you talk about? Did it have to do with the night Garrison Black killed Benton Greene? You were there; I overheard the commissioner say as much to Max."

At the admission, Max's head whipped in Rosemary's direction; by the time his eyes met hers, he had already realized that truly, he shouldn't have been surprised.

His nostrils flared, but he declined to comment, and it turned out he needn't have as Wadsworth said neatly, "One of these days, Miss Rose, you're going to get caught eavesdropping. I pray the person who finds you has half the amount of mercy as I do."

"I second that sentiment," Max agreed, shaking his head.

Rosemary slammed her hand down on the table, and though it didn't make as loud a bang as she'd have liked, the action got her point across. "Enough of this quibbling. Enough secrets. Wadsworth, you will tell me what I want to know because you owe me. You knew about Andrew's illness all along, and you never said a word."

The statement hung in the air, Wadsworth's face contorting into a pained expression. "You're angry with me for keeping something from you, I understand. You're angry with Andrew, and you can't even tell him. But think about this: if you'd known, it would have colored your time with him. You would have lost him still, and you would have been miserable when instead, you were joyous. I'd also like to remind you that your late husband was quite wise—wise enough to consider you his equal and to act as your partner rather than your master. He may have made a mistake, but it was one of very few, in my humble opinion."

Rosemary was forced to consider his words, and while at another juncture, she might have agreed with him, she wasn't ready to completely let it go. "Regardless," she said, locking eyes with Wadsworth and repeated, "You owe me."

It was his turn to consider, which he did for a moment before sighing. "All right, I'll tell you everything, but when I do, we're even."

Rosemary nodded in agreement, and Wadsworth leaned against the table on his forearms, his eyes misting over. "It all began ten years ago, long before Greene was killed when Nathaniel was a new constable. His first murder scene was also Garrison Black's first victim. You won't convince me to describe the details of what we saw, not even with threats, Miss Rose, but suffice it to say, it had an effect on Nathaniel.

"When the second and third murders occurred, he became obsessed with catching Black. The obsession took over his life for that entire year. Nathaniel was young and a bit over-confident. His instincts were some of the best I'd ever seen, which of course, did nothing less than convince him he would always come out with a win in the end.

"It convinced me, as well, and that's why when, after Black's return and second round of murders four years later, I allowed Nathaniel to take the lead. It was my call, and I made the wrong one. We had Black cornered. Constable Turner was our watchman, Nathaniel and I both armed."

Absently, Wadsworth scratched his cheek, fingernails rasping over the stubble of whiskers that gave him a somewhat dangerous look.

"Greene should never have been there, but we needed a third man, and Turner's hands wouldn't stop shaking. Even so, it was three against one. We should have been successful, but things went south. Black had a girl—we didn't know that going in—and I don't know if it was the girl or finally coming face-to-face with the man he'd hunted for four years, but Nathaniel froze. He could have ended Black right then and been done with it. Hesitation cost him the satisfaction of capture, along with something more. Black got a shot off, and Greene went down."

Stoic as he might be, Rosemary could tell the memory pained her butler, but she held back from offering a sympathetic pat on the hand as she thought Wadsworth might not appreciate the gesture.

"But why did Percy call you a coward?" she asked.

"Because I took the blame for Nathaniel's mistake. Turner didn't see what happened, but he heard enough of the aftermath to understand we planned to tell the commissioner an edited story. I almost feel guilty for allowing him to swear silence in the first place. Turner was young and inexperienced, and it wasn't fair of us to put him in that position. Whether you care for his personality or not, Constable Turner isn't a rat. Nor is he a man who breaks his word, although discussing an oath of silence at all is tantamount to breaking it. For that, I'll let him slide, however, given the circumstances."

The longer Max listened, the stormier his eyes grew, and now they were locked onto Wadsworth's in a wordless showdown. Finally, Wadsworth broke the silence.

"Disapprove of my decision all you'd like, but until you've walked in my shoes, as they say, it would behoove you to reserve at least a portion of your presumption. I saved a good officer from being sacked over a moment of rash judgment— one that, quite honestly now that I've had time to reflect—could have happened to any of us. It was a split second of indecision in the face of extreme danger. However, what makes a good leader is understanding and respecting one's subordinates' strengths and weaknesses. I should never have allowed Nathaniel to sway me in the first place. I would have resigned following that poor decision, regardless of it turned out."

This time, Rosemary went ahead and offered the solace of her touch. She tried with only the pressure of her fingers to convey both sympathy and forgiveness for him keeping Andrew's secret. Wadsworth's face reddened slightly, whether out of gratitude or a sense of impropriety was anyone's guess.

He went on, his voice rough with emotion.

"Police work was never for me, no matter how proficient I may have been at the job. I worried that if I continued, someone else would get hurt because of me, and I knew I couldn't live with that. Perhaps I ought to have told the truth, but I stand by my choice. Nathaniel held onto that guilt for six years. It's why he stayed in contact with Margot Greene—as a reminder to never allow over-confidence to get the best of him again. Guilt drove him to become an exemplary officer, and eventually a sergeant, and he made good on his promise to apprehend Black. I'm confident that if he'd lived, Nathaniel would have captured him for the last time."

"Do you believe Black murdered Prescott?" Rosemary asked the question she'd come there to ask.

Wadsworth considered for a moment, hardly the first moment he'd spent pondering that question's answer, Rosemary would wager.

"Based on the nature of the wound, I believe there's a possibility. You've seen Garrison Black's calling card, have you not?"

This time, he addressed himself to Max, who, even as Rosemary nodded, admitted he had.

"Nathaniel spent the years between Black's killing sprees wondering about the significance of the heart. He was convinced the attractive blond targets represented someone important from Black's past—his mother or an unrequited love—someone who hurt him so deeply he felt the need to kill this person again and again."

"A psychological connection," Max fingered his chin thoughtfully.

"Yes," Wadsworth replied. "One Nathaniel hoped to unravel upon Black's capture. It's a shame I hadn't thought to ask him if Black ever confirmed the theory. Nathaniel's conclusions, if not included in his case notes, died with him."

Max's eyebrows scrunched together. "I'd no idea Nate had delved so deeply into Garrison Black's movements and motives. I'm impressed— and further saddened by his loss."

Rosemary stated the obvious, feeling someone ought to. "If this is true, Black is quite mad."

"Many things have driven men to kill without remorse." Wadsworth sounded sad. "Madness is only one. Hatred is another. I find it quite easy to believe that Black would see fit to eliminate anyone who kept him from his mission."

"I'm going to need to take a look at Prescott's case notes, look into Black's past," Max began planning his next move but was quelled by Rosemary's elbow digging into his ribs.

She locked eyes with Wadsworth. "You could tell the commissioner the truth," she implored, Garrison Black's motivation for murder of far less interest than freeing him from a punishment he didn't deserve.

"How would that help, Miss Rose, really?"

"It—it would show that you didn't hate Prescott enough to kill him. That there's no motive." She knew she was wrong the moment the words left her lips. Because he had literally been caught red-handed, no one had bothered to question the motive for Wadsworth to murder Sergeant Prescott in the first place, and yet here he sat.

"Or, perhaps they'll assume I've turned bitter in my time as your butler and resented Nathaniel for putting me in that position. If they want to hang me, they'll hang me one way or another. Find the real killer. I won't sully my friend's name now, and there's nothing you can say to convince me otherwise."

"Would you trot meekly like a lamb to the slaughter before you would speak up for yourself?" Cheeks pinked with fury, Rosemary wagged a finger at Wadsworth. "You're not the man I thought you were."

"I'm a man with faith. Faith in the system of justice for which I once served—faith in Max, and in you." The statement shut Rosemary's mouth with a snap.

"One more thing, Miss Rose," Wadsworth said, his tone as severe as the expression on his face. "When I'm done here—when I'm back where I belong—it all goes back to the way it was between us. If these matters are ever discussed again, I'll submit my resignation. Is that clear?"

Rosemary left Wadsworth to his caged misery, nursed hers in silence on the ride home, and sent Max off with a perfunctory kiss and a promise to be better company on another day.

All she wanted was to mix up a pitcher of G&T and gain the sanctuary of her bedroom, where the quiet would give her a moment to think.

No, that wasn't true at all. What she really wanted, she decided, was to beat the stuffing out of something—anything.

Vera made a handy target when Rosemary heard her laughing with Frederick about running off to Gretna Green.

"You will not." Eyes burning with fury, Rosemary ignored droplets of gin and tonic that splashed as she strode into the parlor. Frederick took one look at his sister, then glanced over to see Vera's answering expression.

"I'll just leave you to it, shall I?" He beat a cowardly retreat that went ignored by the two women.

"I will not what?" Vera began, her mood no less contentious than Rosemary's. "Start my married life the way I choose? I'm not some doe-eyed ingenue still clinging to my mother's apron strings, and you are not my keeper."

"Seems to me you need one. Have you any idea how many excuses I've made for your behavior?"

Rosemary stepped closer to Vera, who had risen to her feet, the better to make her point.

"Did I ask you to make excuses for me?"

"Someone has to, and conveniently, I'm on the spot."

Layered over the heartsick feeling of Andrew's betrayal, Rosemary wouldn't admit, even to herself, she carried some guilt for tattling to her mother regarding Vera and Frederick's imminent living arrangements. Instead of making her feel more charitable, the guilt only fueled Rosemary's ire.

"I'm sorry if my wedding is an inconvenience to you. Rest assured, I only plan to have one, and after this, you won't be troubled again."

So saying, Vera stalked from the room, her footsteps sounding loud on the stairs, but not as loud as when she slammed the door behind her.

Emily Queen

Chapter Seventeen

The next morning Rosemary ate her breakfast in a silent dining room. Of course, Wadsworth was absent; Anna had the day off; and unlike Helen, Gladys didn't seem to feel the need to bang the pots and pans around while she cooked. Frederick had gone to work, and according to the note Vera had hastily scrawled—with no *Love, Vera* at the bottom as she usually would have done—she would be tied up with rehearsals all day.

That Rosemary had a mind like a steel trap and therefore knew good and well rehearsal didn't start until later in the afternoon had either slipped Vera's mind, or she was still stewing over the row they'd had the previous evening.

Rosemary frowned, thinking about it now. In all their years of friendship, she could count on one

214

hand the number of times she and Vera had quarreled, and those arguments had been settled swiftly and with little fanfare. This one would also pass, of that she was confident, but knowing Vera was angry with her still left a bitter taste in Rosemary's mouth, and a feeling of unease that she guessed wouldn't dissipate until she'd made amends.

Furthermore, with no fresh information at their disposal, the newspapers contained little more than a reiteration of the facts trussed up in a slightly different package, and Rosemary threw the pages down in frustration.

"Miss, is there anything I can do for you?" Gladys asked when she entered the dining room and noticed the expression of misery on Rosemary's face. She wrung her hands together as if unsure whether she ought to have asked. The nervous gesture reminded Rosemary that this was a woman who, in the past, had likely lost jobs for less reason than a moment concerned prying.

"No, thank you, Gladys," she replied gently. "I don't think there's much to be done. It seems as though poor Wadsworth has already been tarred and feathered by the press. Each day they become more convinced of his guilt." Tears welled in her eyes and spilled down her cheeks.

Gladys pulled a clean handkerchief from her pocket and handed it to Rosemary. "I'd say he's lucky to have you on 'is side. I'll tell him so m'self when he returns." Her voice turned brusque, almost motherly. "Tis no time for tears, Miss, but rather the time for faith. I've a mind it'll come right in the end."

Rosemary dabbed at her cheeks and smiled blearily. "Thank you, Gladys. That's exactly what I needed to hear." Gladys returned the smile and nodded once, then patted Rosemary on the shoulder and quietly returned to the kitchen.

"Time for faith," Rosemary repeated under her breath, shaking her head. She never had been much good at waiting for things to find her, no matter how skilled she might be at feigning patience. Fortunately, Rosemary didn't have to wait long because the telephone jangled, and a few moments later, she felt a swell of hope as she heard Ivy Gibson's voice come across the line.

"We're meeting today." Ivy sounded flustered. "Did you know? No, of course, you didn't know because I've only just found the stack of notes I meant to send with the time and date."

The invitation was too tempting to pass up, but Rosemary hesitated. She'd half made up her mind to march over to Arabelle Grey's flat and insist upon speaking with the girl. "I didn't know, Ivy. I'll come by, but I won't be able to stay for long. I'm hoping to meet with Miss Grey if she agrees to a conversation."

"That simply won't do. I've assured Esme I would persuade you to attend." Ivy harrumphed and then said, "she asked me specifically to invite you."

Hadn't Ivy been listening? "I've just said I would be there."

"Quite right. Well, then, I've a few more calls to make. I shall look forward to seeing you." Ivy disconnected the line without even a goodbye.

Attending the meeting would help keep her mind off of all her other woes. Feeling somewhat spiteful after their row, she brushed aside the niggling concern that Vera would be positively livid at missing her chance to spend more time with the ladies.

Rosemary readied herself, taking care to don an outfit suited for physical activity this time, and by the time she was finished had decided there was one more thing she needed to do.

Descending the stairs to the studio that once functioned as Andrew's office, Rosemary slid open the middle desk drawer and reached all the way to the back, retrieving the pistol she knew he'd kept there. In the bottom drawer, she found a box of ammunition, which she pocketed along with the gun.

It was better to be safe than sorry, and with Black still on the loose and nobody to accompany her, Rosemary felt just a little safer knowing she could defend herself if necessary.

Thankfully, she wasn't forced to use the pistol on the way to the gymnasium, and by the time she arrived felt a tad silly for having brought it in the first place. She shoved it beneath the driver's seat and hurried inside, expecting to find the day's activities in full swing.

Instead, she was greeted by a circle of women all gathered around something Rosemary couldn't see until she pressed through to the center.

Of all the people in the world Rosemary would have thought she'd see standing arm-in-arm with Esme Prescott, Arabelle Grey would have been last on her list. The sight had Rosemary's head spinning, the pieces of the puzzle of Nathaniel Prescott's murder turning on their edges.

The group was smaller than usual, most likely due to Ivy's unsent missives, but they all wore the same curious expression and eyed Arabelle with speculation. Margot Greene's eyebrow looked as though it were pasted to her hairline as Esme nodded once to Rosemary and proceeded to address the gathering.

"I know you've read the papers and are aware of what has happened. Several of you were at the inquest, and regardless—I've made no secret of my opinion of Miss Grey. However, I am willing to admit I was wrong. Arabelle has experienced a horror the rest of us simply cannot imagine, and I believe taking part in our activities could be of great benefit to her."

Surprise turned to respect on the faces of the ladies, who then turned to Arabelle expectantly.

Shyly—far more shyly than she'd appeared at the fallen heroes banquet—Arabelle cleared her throat before speaking. "Thank you. I would very much like to be part of the group if they'll have me."

A moment of tittering ensued during which Margot Greene appraised Arabelle with hawk-like eyes as if determining her worthiness. Finally, she smoothed her blindingly chartreuse skirt and answered for the group, "You're very welcome, indeed, Miss Grey. You've been through a terrible trial, being attacked in your own home—by the same man who took my son's life, don't forget. If he tries to come for you again, you'll be ready. We'll make sure of it."

Arabelle's admittance having been approved with far less indecision than the level of Esme's fanfare had warranted, Ivy helpfully shifted the conversation to more mundane matters.

Esme took the opportunity, with the bulk of the group distracted, to pull Rosemary and Arabelle through the entrance doors and out into the rear garden area.

"I truly was sincere when I said I was wrong about Arabelle. She isn't the harlot I thought she was," Esme explained furtively, giving the girl's arm a companionable squeeze. "My husband's murderer is still roaming the streets. Perhaps Arabelle knows something of use. She's agreed to speak to you, and I've assured her you're to be trusted as well."

Speaking to Arabelle had been Rosemary's wish for the day. Having Esme grant it for her was a welcome event.

Rosemary turned and assessed Arabelle Grey objectively for the first time. Yes, Arabelle was a beautiful young lady, perhaps twenty-three at most, not really much younger than herself in years.

Yet, there was something else: a vulnerability in her green eyes that reminded Rosemary of Anna, the comparison causing her shamefully to admit she'd previously only paid attention to Arabelle's curvaceous figure and expensive dresses.

Most of her opinion had come from Ivy Gibson's trusted lips. A mistake that Andrew would have pointed out had he been alive to do so.

She could hear his voice in her head. *Remember, Rosie, you should always learn the facts before forming an opinion.*

Realizing Arabelle was on tenterhooks waiting for her to speak, Rosemary reached out and took the girl's hand. "Your secrets will be safe with me."

Arabelle looked searchingly into Rosemary's eyes and, seeming to find what she needed to see, nodded once, and then turned to Esme. "Perhaps you ought to begin by explaining how you came to call on me in the first place. After all, until twenty-four hours ago, you believed me nothing more than a seductress with murderous intent."

There was a rueful lilt to her voice that suggested Arabelle possessed both a sense of humor and an incomparable ability to forgive, driving home the notion that one oughtn't judge a book by its cover.

Esme's face pinked at the comment, but she nodded and began to speak.

"When I arrived back at my hotel following our afternoon at the shooting range, there was a message at the desk—Inspector Whittington informing me I could finally return to my home. It sounds mad, but I thought it would bring some comfort to surround myself with Nate's things. Suffice it to say, I was wrong, and so I turned to the drinks cupboard. Somewhere around my third bourbon, I tore through the study until I found a stack of letters from Arabelle. It's a good thing she wasn't there at that moment; I might have committed murder myself." At that, she tossed another apologetic glance in Arabelle's direction.

"My part of the story stops shortly after that. What I discovered in those letters, well, let's just say it wasn't what I expected. The next morning, I called at Arabelle's flat. I can't imagine why she allowed me inside, but we engaged in a lengthy conversation during which I made my sincerest apologies. After that, Arabelle shared with me some information I believe you'll find quite interesting."

Arabelle opened her mouth, closed it again, and took a few deep breaths. Esme placed a hand on her arm. "It's all right, dear. Take your time. We understand it's a difficult subject. You're accompanied by a group of ladies with enough difficult subjects we ought to have our own shelf at the library."

Esme's encouragement seemed to soothe Arabelle's nerves, and she began, "I never had designs on Sergeant Prescott. Not the kind Esme assumed I did, and now I wish I'd allowed him to tell the truth about our relationship. Nate was like an older brother to me—the one man I knew I could trust with my life. We met six years ago when I was barely a girl. Met isn't exactly the correct word. He saved my life the first time Garrison Black tried to kill me."

For a moment, none of Arabelle's words made sense to Rosemary, and then like the flip of a switch, it all fell into place.

"You were the girl Black almost killed the night Benton Greene died!" she exclaimed.

It was Arabelle's turn to appear stunned. "How did you know? The fact Black took a victim that night was kept from the public."

A blush rising to her cheeks, Rosemary admitted, "I forced Wadsworth to tell me what happened. He didn't reveal your name—only mentioned there had been a girl there that night and that Black had beaten her so badly she barely survived. I'd no idea it was you."

Arabelle's lips pressed together. "Yes, well, as you can see, I've not led the charmed life the public imagines."

That she hadn't spent the last few years secreted away in fear proved there was more to

Arabelle than met the eye. Rosemary experienced another fleeting moment of shame for thinking of the girl uncharitably in the past.

"At the inquest, I thought your butler was the culprit, but now I know my friend and savior could only have been murdered by Garrison Black."

Her choice of words begged the question.

"How can you be certain? Did he confess during your unfortunate incident?"

"No! No." Arabelle assured. "But it fits, does it not? Given the history between us."

Maybe. Maybe not. Rosemary had more questions before she could reach a final conclusion. "Can you tell me what drove you to speak to Sergeant Prescott on the day of his death?" she asked, beginning with the most basic.

Fidgeting with the collar of her dress, Arabelle explained, "Fear—fear is what drove me. As I said before, I've not led a charmed life. In addition to losing my mother and father and being brutalized by Garrison Black, I've been unlucky in love. Too unlucky not to begin wondering whether there might be another explanation for it.

"My aunt and uncle receive a stipend that will end when I marry. It seems they are quite satisfied with their yearly allowance—so satisfied they've sabotaged my every chance at finding a husband and escaping their clutches. I confess I'd come to lean on Mr. Prescott over the years, and I only wanted to ask his advice on how to ensure my current engagement would stick. You see, I'm planning to marry Percy Turner."

Rosemary had to make a conscious effort not to wrinkle her nose, roll her eyes, or outright gag at the thought of Arabelle and Percy together but couldn't quite keep her eyebrow from raising a fraction of an inch. Arabelle didn't misinterpret the meaning behind it.

"I realize he isn't the most handsome man, and perhaps he doesn't make a great first impression, but he's honest, and he's decent. He only lied to protect me, and he's regretted the necessity ever since. Percy would never hurt me, and I know he would protect me with his life," Arabelle explained passionately. "But he doesn't appreciate how underhanded my aunt and uncle can be."

At that moment, the rest of the ladies filed out of the gymnasium, effectively cutting short the conversation. Ivy tossed an apologetic glance in Rosemary's direction.

"It's cold outside." Rosemary couldn't see which lady issued the complaint, but she heartily agreed with the sentiment as Ivy directed the group to begin the session by running in place. Still, the physical activity helped clear her mind as she pondered the implications of what she'd just learned.

"Lift those knees higher," Ivy ordered.

From where she huffed and puffed to keep up with Ivy, Rosemary could see a section of the footpath through the park, and she just happened to be looking in that direction when Betsy Brown passed by.

Seizing the opportunity, not least because it got her out of Ivy's clutches, she muttered an apology to the lady on her right, "If you'll excuse me, there's someone I must speak to."

Chapter Eighteen

If her expeditious exit got her out of a round of calisthenics, Rosemary counted that as a benefit. Further conversation with Arabelle would have to wait, and she couldn't let this fortuitous opportunity pass by unseized.

Somewhere in the depths of her handbag lay the infernal telegram belonging to Betsy, and Rosemary was determined to divest herself of the responsibility of returning it. Good riddance, too. If Vera and Frederick wanted to run off to Gretna Green and get married by a blacksmith, who was she to stop them?

Placating her mother was no reason to ruin a lifelong friendship. Evelyn would forgive the newlyweds eventually, and if Vera wished to antagonize her future mother-in-law over something as trivial as a frock, that was none of Rosemary's affair.

She managed to slip away without drawing Ivy's attention but had to make her way around the gymnasium to get to the footpath. As she rounded the corner, she noticed a dark-clad figure moving furtively towards the park entrance—his eyes locked on Betsy's figure as she disappeared down the path.

As he got closer, the man turned and looked around as if checking to make sure he wasn't being followed, and the sight of his profile made Rosemary stop and gasp. A bushy beard covered part of his face, a tipped-down hat hid the other—but the beard was all she needed to see to know this man was none other than Garrison Black.

Rosemary grappled with what to do next. Should she follow? Find a telephone and ring the police? Was there time for any of that, and what would she do if she caught up with him? She couldn't just turn away, knowing Betsy might be in danger. That wouldn't do at all.

She found it hard to think past the distracting sound of her heartbeat thrumming in her ears, but while she hesitated, Betsy might be running out of time. Max would be furious, but she had to do something, and there wasn't time to call for help.

Ivy had moved the rest of the ladies up the grassy knoll towards the front of the building, out of earshot. Even if she'd wanted to, Rosemary knew involving them would only make matters worse.

Decision made, she sprinted back to her automobile, opened the door, reached beneath the seat, and tucked the pistol into her coat pocket. All she could think of was Betsy as she headed towards the footpath.

No, Betsy wasn't Black's typical type of victim, but if he was Nathaniel Prescott's killer, it wouldn't be the first time he'd broken his pattern. It wasn't up to her to rationalize the actions of a deranged maniac, but it might be up to her to save Betsy's life. With that in mind, Rosemary rounded the first bend and slowed her pace once she recognized the entrance to the overlook Vera had pointed out during their impromptu hike.

There, Betsy stood looking out across the river, her back to the lurking figure, oblivious to the danger he posed. "Look out," Rosemary said, pulling the pistol from her pocket and pointing it at Black.

Wielding that weapon made her feel powerful, but it was also terrifying. Quickly, she realized she didn't relish holding another human being's life in her hands—even one as expendable as Garrison Black's—while at the same time resigning herself to do whatever needed to be done. If, she thought, her hands would only stop shaking.

Betsy whirled, and so did Black, his eyes still not visible beneath the brim of his hat. Rosemary steeled her nerves and prepared to pull the trigger, concerned that at any second, he might produce a weapon of his own.

Instead, he held his hands up in surrender and then pulled his gaze away from Rosemary's gun to rest it on Betsy's face.

"Shoot me if you must, but I'd like one last look at my love before I die." His comment didn't fit into Rosemary's preconceived notion of the situation. It did, however, make sense to Betsy.

"Freddie?" she said, her voice only a breath, yet filled with a hopeful longing so strong and pure Rosemary thought the sun might shove aside the clouds to get a better view.

Betsy walked slowly towards the bearded man who, now that the adrenaline had begun to ebb from Rosemary's system allowing her vision to clear for a better look at his face, only bore a cursory resemblance to Garrison Black.

Curiosity then gave way to sympathy when she noted that above the beard, one side of his face had been horribly disfigured by a mottled scar of the kind only fire could inflict.

"Freddie?" Betsy asked again, her face beginning to crumble as she reached up to place her hand on his cheek. Her eyes searched his, tears welled, then slid slowly down her cheeks. "It is you. I'd know your eyes anywhere."

After that, Rosemary was forced to watch a lengthy embrace that drained the last of her fear and desperation altogether, leaving her impatient and still holding a loaded pistol.

"I'm quite thrilled this seems to have all worked out for you both. However, I believe you owe Betsy an explanation." And if Betsy's Freddie thought Rosemary would leave them in peace to sort things out after the scare he had given her, the man was sorely mistaken.

With less shame than Rosemary would have appreciated, the couple broke apart, and when she'd come back to her senses, Betsy jammed her hands on her ample hips.

"Rosemary is absolutely right. I deserve an explanation. How are you here? You're supposed to be dead."

Freddie seemed to recognize his position was less solid than it had been a few moments ago and tried to collect himself while Rosemary watched with steadily increasing distaste.

"I—I—I made a mistake."

If that wasn't the biggest understatement she'd ever heard, thought Rosemary, she'd eat a shoe.

"Please, Betsy, I made a mistake. I thought you wouldn't love me anymore, looking like, well—" he pulled off one glove to reveal it wasn't only his face that had been scarred. "Like this. I'm a monster. Children cry when they see my face. People whisper and point. I didn't want to force you to live with ridicule for the rest of your life. It's bad enough I have no choice."

He pulled the glove back on with impatient motions.

"And I couldn't bear to see the same look on your face. You'd have tried to hide your dismay because that is the kind of person you are, but the time would come when I would look into your eyes and see the truth."

Betsy's eyes narrowed, and she gestured to her body. "Look at me. Do I look like the same girl you fell in love with? No, I do not. Does that mean you couldn't love me now?"

"Of course not. You're beautiful to me and always will be!" Freddie insisted.

The entire exchange made Rosemary want to vomit. It was so disgustingly mushy it felt like one of Vera's more tragically romantic plays.

Betsy stood, formulating her response amid a silence that drew out long.

"Are you mad?" Rosemary finally shouted. "You sent her a counterfeit telegram so she would think you were dead." She pulled the slip of paper from her pocket and waved it around. "Is that something a rational person does?"

Freddie had the decency to appear chagrined, but only slightly. "I admit, I wasn't in my right mind when I hatched this plot. Mother has never forgiven me. She said the loss of a child was the worst thing a mother could experience and wasn't something to joke about. She was right. I've regretted my choice ever since, but I didn't know how to approach you."

"I don't care what you look like. You're still the man I fell in love with on the inside," Betsy said, apparently unable to keep quiet any longer. "I want to be with you if you still want to be with me."

"I do," Frederick assured her passionately. "I always have. I'll go down to the registry office and marry you right now."

Betsy didn't reply but instead launched herself back into Freddie's arms and resumed kissing as if everything around them had simply disappeared.

"So," Rosemary deadpanned without a sliver of remorse, "does that mean you won't be needing that wedding gown after all?"

Rosemary tossed the telegram to the ground and stomped back up the footpath, all the while shaking her head at the scene she'd just witnessed and muttering to herself. "Of all the absurd endings to a story…idiotic idea, faking one's own death…inconsiderate rotter, if he were my beau, I'd have thrown him into the river."

The pistol felt heavy in her pocket now, and she couldn't wait to return it to its resting place in Andrew's study. How stupid to have brought it along in the first place, she thought. She could have killed an innocent man and wound up even worse off than Wadsworth. He at least had the sense and sensibility to remain calm in the face of a crisis.

What was it Nathaniel Prescott had said during his speech at the fallen heroes banquet? Something about how no person was infallible. It was good advice from a good man who had been taken from the world all too soon.

She supposed she ought to grant Freddie Poole the same amount of understanding, but she was still too angry to do so. He'd hurt Betsy with his lie, and from the sounds of it hadn't done his mother any favors, either.

That Betsy was able to instantly forgive made her one of two things: either far more magnanimous than Rosemary or far more daft. Either way, she decided to thoroughly learn her lesson and refrain from casting judgment.

Her thoughts returning to Sergeant Prescott for a reason she couldn't quite put her finger on, Rosemary tried to remember the rest of his eloquent speech. She'd been so distracted by Percy Turner's rude remarks and Ivy Gibson's commentary that much of the ceremony had become a blur.

He'd been peering intently at Margot Greene, that much she remembered, and his eyes had been filled with emotion. *We must take responsibility for our actions—and, more importantly, for our mistakes.* Prescott's words came back to her in a rush, and knowing what she knew now, took on new meaning.

That he'd carried his guilt with him to his grave was a sad thought, indeed. Benton Greene's death was tragic, surely, and perhaps could have been avoided. Unfortunately, there was no comprehensive manual for confronting and capturing a spree killer, and only the fates knew whether it had merely been Greene's time to go.

Rosemary stopped in her tracks and gasped as all the clues fell neatly into place.

As Freddie Poole had so helpfully pointed out, losing a child was the worst thing a mother could experience. Certainly enough to drive a woman to seek justice—or, as the case may be—revenge.

Something in her gut told Rosemary she was right: Margot Greene had murdered Sergeant Nathaniel Prescott.

CHAPTER NINETEEN

Rosemary remained frozen for a few more moments while the realization set in, and she mentally ran through the evidence. Margot Greene could easily have visited the Prescott residence the day the sergeant was killed. She'd been on friendly terms with both Esme and Nathaniel, and it wasn't out of the realm of possibility that she was familiar with the layout of their home.

Certainly, Margot knew how to operate a gun, and though she hadn't stated outright that she owned one, her mention of the grey squirrel garden invasion left little doubt that she did.

Lastly, and most importantly, Nathaniel Prescott had played a role in the death of Margot's only son. He'd been distraught, his guilt mounting after being bestowed with a pay raise and a new rank he felt he might not entirely deserve.

How Margot had figured it out, Rosemary wasn't sure, but she suspected Prescott's speech at the fallen heroes banquet had been a factor. Margot's demeanor towards him had seemed to shift throughout the evening, and Rosemary recalled thinking she wasn't quite as taken with Prescott as Ivy Gibson had indicated.

Margot had then left the banquet with Percy Turner, and it occurred to Rosemary that perhaps he had let something slip, adding fuel to her fire. Whether Wadsworth believed Percy an honorable officer or not, Rosemary still hadn't forgiven him for his comments regarding herself and Max. It would suit her nicely to have an excuse to vilify him—at this point, she would believe Percy responsible for everything from the fly in her teacup to the collapse of the Roman empire—but it hardly mattered now.

What did matter was ensuring Margot Greene got what was coming to her.

Rosemary broke into a run for the second time that day, retracing her steps back to the gymnasium while attempting to formulate a plan. If she played her cards right, she could keep Margot occupied long enough to summon Max, force a confession, and have Wadsworth home for dinner.

The ladies had finished exercising by the time she arrived at the back door. Some of the autos parked nearby had gone, but the presence of a bright green touring car told Rosemary Margot likely was among the stragglers, and she felt relieved to know she wasn't too late.

Upon entering the gymnasium, she breathed another sigh of relief and thanked her lucky stars. Margot had indeed hung back, along with Esme, Ivy, and Arabelle, though as she hoisted the strap of her petit point purse onto her shoulder, it appeared she was poised to depart.

"Ivy," Rosemary hissed, summoning the woman to her side. "Is there a working telephone in this building?"

Ivy quirked a brow and answered, "Yes, why? What's wrong?"

"I need you to remain calm. Go, find the telephone as fast as you can, and ring Max at the station. Tell him Margot Greene murdered Nathaniel Prescott, and give him this address. Quickly, and don't make a fuss, or she'll escape."

Ivy's hands shook, but she did as she was told and pasted a smile on her face that even Rosemary almost believed.

All that was left to do was keep Margot occupied until Max arrived. Perhaps a bit of pressing from the chief inspector would prompt her to come clean, and if not, at least in the meantime, he could have her home searched for the murder weapon.

Rosemary watched Margot converse with the woman whose husband she'd murdered in cold blood and felt her stomach turn over once more at the audacity. A few scant moments later, Ivy reappeared, only slightly breathless from her trip to the phone and back, and nodded shortly in confirmation to Rosemary. Knowing Max was on his way and that for once, she might be able to avoid a showdown with a deranged murderer, made her feel a little better.

It occurred to her later she oughtn't to have allowed herself even a moment of relief. Perhaps she'd been cursed with bad luck, or perhaps she was simply a magnet for trouble.

Fortified by Ivy's presence, Rosemary approached the three ladies just in time to hear

Margot announce it was getting late, and she ought to be off. Being possessed of quick wit and sly tongue, Rosemary should have been able to come up with a dozen ways to stall Margot. Not a single one came to mind.

"I'm afraid I can't let you do that," Rosemary said, blocking her way towards the exit.

Margot blanched and demanded, "Whyever not?"

"I think you know why. The police are on their way to arrest you for the murder of Nathaniel Prescott." Rosemary glanced towards Esme, wishing she had been able to break the news to her new friend in a less blunt manner.

One hand fluttering to her throat, Esme uttered a strangled cry, reached out with her other hand to clutch Arabelle's arm tightly enough to leave marks on her skin that wouldn't fade for days. Arabelle barely noticed as she stared at Margot with shock-widened eyes.

"That's absurd," Margot huffed, trying to press past Rosemary, who refused to budge an inch. Ivy linked arms with her, forcing Margot to take a step back. She glanced at those who blocked her path and denied the accusation again. "Mr.

Prescott was a friend to me. I would never have done anything to hurt him. He—he—that's absurd!"

Her voice had become more shrill, and her eyes wilder as it became clear nobody in the room was buying what she was attempting to sell.

"Are you certain?" Ivy demanded. Rosemary nodded, which was all Ivy needed to see. Her mouth set in a grim line, she settled her weight more deeply into the balls of her feet, her whole body tensed in preparation to fight if such was needed.

"Why, Margot?" Arabelle was the one to ask since Esme seemed unable to find her voice through the lump of betrayal that had risen in her throat.

Margot declined to respond, instead pursing her lips and crossing her arms resolutely.

"Because," Rosemary answered for her, "She blamed Nathaniel for her son's death. Pure and simple vengeance, wasn't it, Margot?"

This seemed to press a button Rosemary hadn't known existed, but she finally got what she wanted when Margot exclaimed, "Not vengeance!

It was justice! Justice not only for my poor, sweet Benton's death—but for me! For the last six years, I've been made a fool. He let me believe he was my friend, all the while, knowing he'd taken my boy from me. I did feel sorry for you, of course," she directed at Esme, "and I almost came clean at the inquest when your maid pointed her finger in my direction. But then, as if by providence, it turned out her accusation was actually for Miss Grey. I took it as a sign I'd done the right thing, and I stand by it now."

"Say his name," Esme said quietly, but with a warning edge to her voice. "Say the name of the man you murdered. The man you took from me in what you mistakingly believe to be *justice*."

"Nathaniel," Margot spat. "I killed Nathaniel Prescott. I didn't plan it that way, mind you. I went to him because of what he'd said at the banquet. The way he looked at me when he spoke of taking responsibility for one's actions—it rankled.

"For two days, I wondered what he meant by that, and finally, I couldn't take it any longer. Nobody was home when I arrived, so I let myself in through the front door and found him at his desk.

I asked if he was responsible for Benton's death, and he said, "yes." It was all I needed to hear.

"Fortunately, I'd my pistol in my handbag. I didn't even think twice before I pulled the trigger. And now, if you ladies don't step aside, I won't think twice about pulling it again."

Margot reached for the handbag still slung over her shoulder, and Rosemary's opinion as to whether or not she ought to have brought Andrew's pistol did a 180-degree turn. She drew her own weapon from her coat pocket quicker than Margot could.

"I wouldn't if I were you," she said. "You're not the only marksman in the room."

Her hands rising in surrender, Margot backed down and dropped the handbag. "Let's not make any hasty decisions now," she said, backing away.

"Why not?" Esme demanded. "You certainly did. You pulled the trigger before you learned the whole story. Your son's death was an accident, not cold-blooded murder."

Margot scoffed, but Arabelle would have none of it. "I was there that night. I was one of Black's victims—the only one to survive, but barely. Black had me by the hair, the gun pressed to my chest. I thought I was going to die, and then my saviors arrived.

"Nate had Black in his sights, his gun aimed and ready to fire, but Black was too quick for him. He used me as a shield, and Nate hesitated before taking a shot. Your son lunged, attempting to take Black down, but he wasn't fast enough. Instead of pursuing Black, Nate rushed to your boy's side. He tried to save him, but it was too late. If you want to blame someone, blame Garrison Black."

Arabelle's description had little effect on Margot. In fact, she scoffed and turned to Esme. "Now you believe the little minx? That's quite convenient, isn't it? It's a pity she hadn't spent a few moments more with your husband. Then, I could have killed two birds with one stone."

The color rose from Esme's neck all the way up to her forehead, a dull red that even touched the tips of her ears. A snarl escaped her lips, and she looked poised to attack. Esme lunged, but not in Margot's direction, instead yanking the gun from Rosemary's fingers. Before Margot could reach for her handbag, Esme had her in her sights.

"Esme, no!" Rosemary cried. "Think of Wadsworth! You'll both be hanged, and she'll have got away with it all!"

"She killed my husband, and she'd kill the lot of us if she thought it would help her now," Esme said miserably and thumbed the hammer back, the metallic click sounding like doom.

Rosemary looked to Ivy for support, but that normally-capable lady appeared frozen in dismay. Arabelle alone kept her wits, although Rosemary questioned her level of sanity when she took a step closer to the gun-wielding woman who had, until quite recently, despised her almost as much as she despised Margot Greene now.

"Esme," Arabelle said calmly. "You know Nate wouldn't have wanted you to take a life on his account. Remember what he said at the banquet. *We must continue to remain vigilant, to expect more from ourselves and each other, and to take responsibility for our actions—and more importantly, for our mistakes.*"

Gently, she tugged on Esme's arm. "Her son sacrificed himself for me. She deserves to die, but not by your hand. Don't turn Benton's noble act into a catalyst for more tragedy. She's not worth the cost of a hanging rope."

Esme dropped her arm and allowed Rosemary to retrieve the pistol. And then, just moments before Max, accompanied by Constable Turner, burst through the doors, Esme marched across the floor and punched Margot Greene squarely in the nose—twice.

CHAPTER TWENTY

Late evening found Rosemary pacing the parlor while the sullen pair of Vera and Frederick listened to her tale of intrigue and woe. During the telling of Margot Greene's capture, Vera's eyes turned stormy and dark with little specks of flickering gold that, to Rosemary's mind, looked too much like fire for her liking.

"She's been arrested, and Max assures me the case is a lock. The best she can hope for is a plea of insanity, but it's rather a doubtful outcome. And so, we'll have Wadsworth back as soon as Max can finish the paperwork. Isn't that great news?"

Vera's lips pursed tightly for a moment before she shifted in her chair, crossing one leg over the other, and stared at her friend with those stormy eyes. "Of course it's great news, Rosemary," she said acidly, "It's the best news I've heard in weeks."

Now she stood, gathered to her full height, and towering two inches above Rosemary even as her calm demeanor evaporated. "You put yourself in danger, got to be a hero again, and you didn't include me!" Vera stomped one foot at the end of her statement, the action combined with the pout of her lips causing her to look exactly like a child throwing a temper tantrum.

"Us, Vera. She didn't include *us*," Frederick interjected.

Vera shot him a look that caused him to shut his mouth with an audible click of his teeth and continued to rant. "You're leaving me behind! I'll be stuck with only Fred from now on, while you're off having fun and solving murders!"

"Hey!" Frederick hollered indignantly, his outburst duly ignored.

"Solving murders is hardly fun!" Rosemary snapped back. "Where's the thank you for not putting your life in danger? And you're the one insisting on running down the aisle to tie yourself to Freddie for the rest of your life. If that's not what you want, then give him back the ring!"

At this, Frederick jumped to his feet and turned on his sister, shouting, "Rosemary!" loud enough for the neighbors next door to hear.

She waved him off with a flick of her wrist. "Go away, Fred, this doesn't concern you."

"Doesn't concern me? You two have gone positively mad! Perhaps I ought to be the one to take the ring back. Perhaps I ought to be done with the both of you!" He stomped out of the parlor, slamming the door behind him, his exit not having quite the effect he'd hoped for given neither Vera nor Rosemary even bothered to glance in his direction.

"I'm not leaving you behind, Vera," Rosemary snapped. "You're the one who can't think of anything except Frederick and your precious wedding plans anymore! You've nearly killed my mother, and now you've started in on me."

Barbs flung between the pair for quite some time before the sound of a throat being cleared cut through the silence left when both women were forced to stop and take a breath.

Rosemary spun around, all thoughts of the fight forgotten in an instant, for she knew what throat the noise had come from. She'd heard it so many times, and missed it so much it felt like Easter, Christmas, and New Year's Eve all rolled into one.

"Wadsworth!" she exclaimed, veritably flying across the room where she flung her arms around him, Vera at her heels. "Oh, Wadsworth, I'm so sorry!" they chorused.

He patted both of their backs somewhat woodenly, and when neither immediately let go said, "Ehem, Madam, Miss Vera."

When they'd extricated themselves, he clasped his hands behind his back. "I wanted to know if there was any pressing business before I turn in for the night. Gladys has kindly informed me that the kitchen is in tip-top shape. I'm quite grateful for that." His tone indicated it was she who he was grateful for, and by extension, Helen's departure.

Rosemary smiled but internally rolled her eyes. Wadsworth had, apparently, been quite serious when he'd said he wanted their relationship to remain precisely as it had been before his arrest and incarceration. However, she did detect a misty quality in his eyes that belied those words but decided not to press him on the issue.

"All that is to be done is for you to join us in a toast. I do insist," she added before he could protest.

The next morning, Rosemary woke feeling more at peace than she had in weeks despite having managed only a few hours of sleep. Instead, she'd spent much of the night perusing Andrew's remaining journals and had happened upon a passage that put her anger to rest.

"Tonight is the night. As much as it will kill me to speak the words aloud, I have to come clean. Rosemary will realize something isn't right, and she'll simply pry it out of me anyway. I suppose I've been reluctant to admit the truth, even to myself, but Rosemary deserves my honesty. She must be allowed to prepare herself for the inevitable, no matter how much it will pain me to see her suffer."

Knowing it had been difficult for him to keep his secret was enough to quell her fear that he'd hidden anything else of import. Reading his words and remembering the love they'd shared was still painful, but it was no longer the raw wound she had bore since his passing.

When Rosemary arrived in the dining room for breakfast, Vera attempted a glare that came off, at the most, as half-hearted. Though Wadsworth remained silent, stationed near the kitchen door, as usual, his presence alone precluded any notion of continuing the argument from the previous evening.

Frederick, who rarely let anything trouble him for more than an evening anyway, greeted her with a rousing recitation of the morning's headlines. *"Local woman, Margot Greene, confesses to the murder of Sergeant Nathaniel Prescott. Carrington Wadsworth released from police custody!"*

Wadsworth's expression didn't waver at the mention, but he exited quietly to the kitchen in silent protest.

"Thank goodness it's all over," Vera said when he'd gone.

Rosemary cocked an eyebrow. "Garrison Black is still on the loose. It isn't all over just yet."

Vera waved a hand dismissively. "I've faith Max will capture him in due time, but for now,

Freddie and I can get back to deciding where and when we're going to be married."

Before Rosemary could work herself into a frenzy at the comment, the doorbell rang, and Max was ushered into the dining room. "There's a rather large package on your doorstep," he declared. "Wadsworth is fetching it now."

A large package it was, indeed, and Rosemary's worries were quelled when she scanned the attached note.

"You'll be getting married in Pardington," she informed Vera, "exactly as planned. As it turns out, Betsy Brown is more charitable than I'd given her credit for. Take a look."

Vera let out a screech, banished Frederick from the dining room before he could catch a glimpse, and buried herself in satin and tulle. "Thank you, Rosie! You're the greatest friend one could ever hope for!"

"I'll remember that the next time you're cross with me," Rosemary replied wryly, turning her attention to Max.

"Have you time for a stroll?" She asked, hopefully. "It's been ages since we've had chance to discuss anything other than murder. I'll even let you hold my hand to stave off the chill."

Max grinned widely. "That's the best offer I've had all week."

"Just all week?" Rosemary teased.

"Rosemary Lillywhite, it's the best offer I've had for my entire life."

-The End-

Made in the USA
Las Vegas, NV
09 April 2024